The Hardy Boys®
in
Revenge of the Desert Phantom

Hardy Boys® Mystery Stories in Armada

* For contractual reasons, Armada has been obliged to publish from No. 57 onwards before publishing Nos. 41–56. These missing numbers will be published as soon as possible.

The Hardy Boys® Mystery Stories

Revenge of the Desert Phantom

Franklin W. Dixon

Armada

First published in the U.S.A. in 1985 by Wanderer Books,
a divison of Simon & Schuster Inc.
First published in Armada in 1987 by
Fontana Paperbacks,
8 Grafton Street, London W1X 3LA

Armada is an imprint of
Fontana Paperbacks, part of
the Collins Publishing Group

Printed in Great Britain by
William Collins Sons & Co. Ltd, Glasgow

Contents

1 Mantu

"Ba-bop-ba-dop . . . bee-boop-ba-dop."

With one hand on the steering wheel, seventeen-year-old Joe Hardy used his free hand to tap out dance steps on the dashboard with his fingers. "Ba-bop-ba-dop . . . bee-boop-ba-dop . . . boop-boop-ba-do-bop. . . . That's it!," he said to himself, completing the musical phrase as he swung the yellow convertible into the driveway. "Ba-bop-ba-dop . . ."

"Earth to Joe! Earth to Joe! Come in, Joe!"

The blond sleuth caught his fingers in mid-high-kick and looked up. He'd been too absorbed in what he was doing to even notice his brother, Frank, who was standing in the driveway staring at him like he'd lost his mind. Dark-haired and a year older than Joe, Frank was the less wild of the two amateur detectives. He tended to think things through before acting. Joe tended to act first and think later. They made a good team.

Joe rolled down the car window and gave his brother a sheepish grin. "Uh, hi. I didn't see you."

"I guess not!" The older boy laughed. "What were you doing?"

"Just working out a song-and-dance routine for Iola. She's entering the Barmet Bay Beauty Pageant and wants me to choreograph her routine for the finals. Pretty neat, huh?"

Iola Morton was Joe's girlfriend. She was also one of the best-looking girls at Bayport High, and Joe had talked her into entering the annual beauty contest, figuring she was a cinch to win.

"Here, look at these steps I worked out for her," the blond boy went on, starting to go over the routine again with his fingers.

"Forget the stupid dance steps!" Frank interrupted as he suddenly remembered what had been on his mind.

It dawned on Joe that his brother didn't just happen to be standing in the driveway but had run out of the house the second he'd driven in. "Is something wrong?"

"No! Something's right!" Frank spoke excitedly. "I think we've got a new case! A big one! We're supposed to leave for Paris in the morning!"

Joe's jaw dropped a little. "Paris? A case? What?"

"Come on inside and I'll show you. Some African guy called Mantu came by today. He wants us to locate a girl for him and he thinks she might be in Paris."

Joe climbed from the convertible and followed his brother, who had started back toward the house. "What's the problem? Is she a runaway or something?" he asked, wondering what had Frank so hopped up. Missing-persons cases were the dregs of detective work, often tedious and rarely fruitful.

"Not just a runaway. This is major stuff. Her father was the president of a small African nation called Zebwa, and now they want her to take over the presidency!"

Joe blew a low whistle as they entered the front hall. "Sounds big all right."

"It is. Her name is Niki Jerusa. Here's a picture of her. It was taken four years ago. She should be about our age by now."

Frank picked a photograph off the hall table and handed it to his brother. It was worn and cracked, like it had been carried around in a wallet for years. The image was of a young and very pretty African schoolgirl.

"Looks like a junior-high-school yearbook picture," Joe mused, his curiosity now piqued. "Who's this guy looking for her? You said his name was Mantu?"

"Right. He's from Zebwa himself," Frank said and nodded. "I called Dad in New York to check out his story. He said he'd put Radley on it and call back around six."

The sleuths' father, Fenton Hardy, was one of the best private detectives in the business and was presently at his New York City office working on a case. Sam Radley was one of Mr. Hardy's chief operatives.

"If Dad says Mantu's story is on the level," Frank went on, "we'll be on our way to Paris tomorrow. Mantu says he picked up a good lead there."

Having all but forgotten about Iola and the beauty pageant, Joe again squinted at the faded photo. "I still don't get it," he said, looking befuddled. "You mean some strange guy called Mantu just showed up out of the blue at our doorstep and . . . ?"

Frank laughed, suddenly realizing that he'd successfully thrown his younger brother into a state of total and complete confusion. "Sorry, I guess I haven't been making much sense," he replied. "Come on, let's sit down and take it from the top."

Joe breathed an exaggerated sigh of relief. "Good."

The boys went into the living room where a set of blueprints lay scattered over the coffee table and sofa. The blueprints were of the interior layout for the "super van" they'd been saving for, and Frank had spent the better part of the day at home going over the sketches. Their dream van would be equipped with the latest electronic surveillance and detection gear—including a computer with a modem tie-in to police computer files. But Frank and Joe were still a long way from being able to afford it.

"I was home alone when this big African guy comes to the door and says his name is Mantu," the dark-haired boy began, flopping down on the sofa. "He was easily six feet tall, carried a briefcase, and had these really intense coal-black eyes. I thought he was looking for Dad at first, but he tells me he's looking for us and shows me this picture of Niki. He said he'd been tracking her down for months with no luck, and now he has to go back to Zebwa and wants us to take up the search for him."

"In Paris?" Joe asked.

Frank nodded. "He was here in the States on a lead, but it turned out to be a dead end. He thinks she's still in Paris, where he said he'd done most of his looking."

"What made him pick us?"

"Just said he'd heard about our reputation as hot-shot detectives," the older boy said and grinned proudly. "Anyway, Zebwa is a small nation in central Africa, and Niki's father, Ben Jerusa, was its president. But about two years ago there was a revolution there. A rebel faction known as the Totas

11

took over the capital city and stormed the presidential palace. They assassinated Niki's father. Many of Jerusa's followers were also killed, but others escaped into the jungle—including Niki."

"I think I remember reading something about that in the newspaper," Joe remarked. "The Totas were supposed to be a rough bunch, weren't they?"

"And they still are. It's pretty much a military state now, and Mantu said they often resort to torture to keep the people in line."

The blond boy shuddered. "Sounds grim. I guess Niki's lucky she made it out of there alive."

"If you can say that a girl who lost her family and her country is lucky, yes." Frank shrugged. "Her mother died years before and her father was all she had left. Apparently, she's been alone and on the run ever since the revolution took place two years ago."

"So who is Mantu and why does he want her now?"

"Well, it seems that many of the Jerusa loyalists have regrouped since the Tota takeover and are planning to make a bid to regain power. Mantu is one of these loyalists and has been sent by their leader to locate Niki. With her, he says they stand a much better chance of rallying the people's support. The Zebwanians loved President Jerusa and loved Niki as well. To have her as a figurehead for their cause would be invaluable in inspiring the people to take up arms against the Totas. The people are afraid to fight the rebels, but to have a Jerusa leading them would give them the courage to do it, anyway."

Joe knit his brow, then stood up and began pacing back and forth over the living-room floor. "Makes sense. But how do we know we can trust Mantu's story? And how come he came to us? That seems a little weird."

"I know. That's why I called Dad to check it out. I also spent most of the afternoon researching Zebwa at the library. So far his story does check out. But I want to hear what Dad has to say. He'd said he'd call at six."

The blond youth glanced at his watch. "It's five to six now."

"Your watch must be off," Frank said, looking at a clock on the wall. "That says twenty of."

Joe stopped pacing and gazed at the electric wall clock in the living room. "I set my watch this morning. If anything's wrong, it's the clock. . . ." Joe's face suddenly twisted up in thought and he gazed at his brother, who was apparently having the same thought. "Come on, let's check out the other clocks," he said, heading back toward the hall.

Without another word, both boys began to inspect other electric clocks in the house. All read twenty until six, including the one in the kitchen, where they found their mother busily fixing dinner.

"Hi, Mom." Frank smiled, giving Laura Hardy a kiss on the cheek. "All the clocks around here are

13

slow. Was there a power failure sometime this afternoon?"

Mrs. Hardy's bright blue eyes sparkled. "No, it was just the circuit breaker. It must've blown while Gertrude and I were out shopping and you were at the library. I guess we forgot to correct the clocks."

Gertrude was Mr. Hardy's sister, who was on one of her frequent extended visits to the Hardy household. The stern, angular woman had taken some getting used to at first, but over time the boys had grown to love their aunt, and like her a lot, too.

Frank focused on the kitchen door. Small splinters of wood had been chipped off next to the knob. Stooping down, he studied the lock for a moment before standing again. "I was afraid of this. This lock's been jimmied. Somebody must have broken in here this afternoon and flipped the breaker switch to cut off the alarm."

"You mean a burglar was in here?" Laura gasped.

Frank sighed. "That's what it looks like, Mom. We'd better see what's missing."

The brothers searched the house, but found nothing out of place. The only room they didn't check was the upstairs bathroom, where Aunt Gertrude was in the process of setting her hair.

"Maybe we should ask Gertrude if she found anything of hers gone," Joe suggested, befuddled over the fact that the burglar hadn't stolen anything.

Frank rolled his eyes. "If she noticed anything gone, we'd all have known about it long ago. But

14

you're right. We'll ask her to check through her stuff when she's finished in the bathroom."

"Yeah, like in a couple of hours?" the blond boy chuckled.

Wondering what the intruder could have been after, Frank and Joe headed back to the kitchen to report the good news to their mother. But they were stopped en route by the ringing of the hall phone. Joe picked it up.

It was Mr. Hardy.

"Everything Mantu told you seems to check out," the famous detective's voice came over the line. "Zebwa was overthrown by Tota rebels two years ago, and now the Jerusa loyalists have gathered in the mountains with a small force behind them. Their leader's name is Akutu, a former top general in Jerusa's army. It makes sense that he would want Niki Jerusa back among them to help rally the support of the people. The Totas are known to be cruel and merciless fanatics with little regard for human rights or the welfare of the people. The United Nations supports anything that can be done to put the Jerusa loyalists back in power."

"Then you think we should take the case?" Joe asked eagerly.

Fenton took some time to form his thoughts before answering. "Here's what I think," he finally responded. "I don't know why Mantu's chosen you two for this mission, but I think you should take the case and do all you can to find this Niki girl. But if

15

you do find her, make sure she agrees to Mantu's plan before you turn her over to him. She's evidently gone to great lengths not to be found, and she may have reasons which none of us . . ."

The boys' famous father stopped speaking, suddenly interrupted by what sounded like a rain storm coming over the line. "Is it raining up there?" he asked after a moment.

Suddenly, the rain noise stopped—not with a click, but muffled, as if someone's hand had just been squeezed over a mouthpiece.

"Check the bathroom," Mr. Hardy said, quickly deducing the source of the sound.

Joe set the receiver down and started up the hall stairs to the second floor.

"What are you doing?" Frank called after him.

"Follow me! Hurry!"

Reaching the upstairs hall, the two boys found their aunt standing outside the bathroom door, in her bathrobe and her hair up in curlers.

"Who's in there?" Joe asked.

"I thought it was one of you two!" the woman responded, surprised to see her nephews. "I was just preparing to use the shower myself. It must be Laura."

"Mom's in the kitchen," Joe stated, trying the bathroom door and finding it locked. "Stand back."

"Then who . . . ?" Gertrude yelped as the blond boy gave the door a karate kick and it flew open.

The bathroom was empty. The shower was run-

16

ning. The window was wide open. And a cordless phone lay on the tile floor.

Frank and Joe ran to the window and looked out at the same moment the burglar alarm began to sound. They scanned the back yard, but no one was visible.

"That guy who broke in was hiding here all afternoon!" Frank deduced, staring out at the empty yard.

"What guy?" Aunt Gertrude demanded, trying to keep her composure.

"Somebody broke into the house when we were all out this afternoon. He must've been hiding up here the whole time!"

"You mean some strange man was hiding in the shower while I was fixing my hair?" Gertrude shrieked, her composure now gone.

"That's what it looks like," Frank said and winked at his ruffled relative. "But I'm sure he was a very nice man."

"Nice man?!" Gertrude cried, advancing on the boys. "I'll *nice man* you, you little . . . !"

Bounding back down the stairs to escape their aunt's fury, the boys first made a short stop on the landing to shut off the alarm-system control. Then they returned to the hall phone to report to their father. But report what?

Frank took the receiver this time. "He had that cordless phone from your bedroom, Dad. He must've been hiding upstairs all afternoon, slipping

17

from room to room to avoid detection and finally ending up behind the shower curtain in the bathroom while Gertrude was fussing with her hair and we were searching the place."

"What was the shower doing on?" Fenton Hardy queried.

"Oh, Gertrude left the bathroom for a minute, and when she came back the intruder must've locked the door and turned on the shower to make her think someone was in it. I guess he forgot to put his hand over the mouthpiece to block out the noise."

This still left the big question unanswered. Motive. Why had the intruder gone to such lengths to eavesdrop on the Hardy household?

"I'll bet this ties in with Mantu," Frank spoke into the receiver.

"It's a good bet," his father agreed. "And it might mean someone other than Mantu has his own reasons for wanting to find Niki Jerusa."

Frank dug into his pocket and drew out the photograph of the pretty thirteen-year-old girl. "I know. And it makes it all the more imperative we find her before someone else does."

Just then, someone knocked on the front door.

2 Purple Hair

"Gotta go, Dad. Someone's at the door. I'll call before we make any moves." Frank hung up the phone and turned toward the front door to find his brother gawking at a pretty teenaged girl in a strapless yellow satin evening gown, white silk gloves, and high heels.

"You'd think I had purple hair or something," she said and rolled her eyes at Joe's gaping mouth. "Are you going to let me in, or would you prefer staring at me like that all evening?"

It was Joe's girlfriend, Iola.

"Uh, sure," the blond boy stammered. "Come on in."

Iola's usual attire was blue jeans and a sweat shirt, so it took a few seconds for the brothers to adjust to this vision of loveliness. The pretty strawberry blonde swished inside like a model showing off the latest fashion.

"Well, how do you like it?" she said and smiled.

"It's . . . it's great!" Frank answered for his awestruck brother. "Is that what you're wearing for the beauty contest?"

"Yup. I just thought I'd try it out on you guys first."

Joe winced, having forgotten all about the contest, which was only three days away. "Uh, maybe that contest wasn't such a good idea," he spoke timidly. "Maybe we should just bag it."

"Well, thanks a lot!" Iola exclaimed sarcastically. "You take one look at me and decide to call it off. I happen to think I look pretty snappy!"

"I didn't mean that. I only meant . . ."

"How do you like that?" the girl sniffed, turning to Frank. "This was his idea in the first place!"

"It's not you!" Joe nearly shouted, trying to get a word in. "You look great! It's just that a case came up and we have to go to Paris tomorrow, so I won't be around to help you with your act. I'm sorry."

"Oh, so it's another case?" Iola pouted. "What is it this time? Space sabotage? Voodoo gangsters? Hamster thieves?"

"It's a missing girl. And it's really important that we find her."

"And I suppose I'm not important?"

Feeling hurt but not wanting to show it, Iola turned away, blinking back the tears which were beginning to form in her eyes. Joe quickly wrapped his arm around her satiny waist. "Of course you're important," he said soothingly. "You know that. Anyway, half the reason you love me is because I'm such a hot-shot detective," he added with a wink, using the same description of their talents Frank had used earlier. "Right?"

Unconsoled, Iola broke from Joe's grasp. "Love *schmove*. You got me started on this and I'm going to see it through. I want that scholarship."

First prize was a full college scholarship, and the pretty high-school junior was determined to win it.

Frank sighed inwardly at the teenaged couple, knowing the strain their detective work could put on a relationship. He'd often had such arguments with his own girlfriend, Callie Shaw, who felt he cared more about solving mysteries than being with her. "What about Chet?" he offered. "Couldn't he help you with your routine?"

Chet Morton was both Iola's big brother and the Hardys' best friend.

"I know Chet won't do it," the strawberry blonde said with a frown. "He'll think it's sissy stuff. I'm going to ask the one person I know who'll both be around and be happy to help—Jim Gunther."

Iola spoke the name with an inflection which left no doubt that it was meant to upset Joe. Jim

21

Gunther was a classmate of Joe's who'd been trying to steal Iola away for the past year, constantly asking her to go on dates with him and hoping she'd give in. She hadn't, but she'd always kept Jim in the back of her mind if Joe started treating her like excess baggage. And that's how she felt right now.

Joe winced. "Come on, you're just saying that because you're mad. You know what Gunther is really after."

"That's right, and I know what I'm *really* after, too!" Iola retorted, stepping to the door. "A scholarship! Have fun in gay Paree!"

With that, Iola strutted out, slamming the door behind her as she went.

Frank slung a brotherly arm across Joe's shoulder. "She'll get over it," he said, trying to cheer him up. "Right now we have more important things to worry about—like saving small African nations!"

"I *hope* she gets over it," the blond sleuth groaned. "She sure looked terrific in that outfit."

"Why don't you call her when we get to Paris? Ask her what kind of French perfume she'd like?"

Joe lit up. "Now you're thinking," he said with a grin, snapping out of his gloom.

Joe didn't stop worrying about Iola until the following morning, when Mantu appeared at the door.

"Good day! I am Mantu. I suppose your brother has told you all about me?"

Joe carefully scrutinized the stranger, trying to

22

size him up. The tall African was just as Frank had described him, about six foot three and wearing a brightly patterned gold-and-green African tribal shirt. But his eyes almost defied description. His irises were so dark that they could barely be discerned from his pupils, so dark that they looked like orbs of solid black coal floating in two sockets. If a man can be fathomed by looking into his eyes, Mantu was the exception. His eyes were impenetrable walls.

"Yes, he did." Frank returned the smile as he joined his brother at the door. "And we've decided to take the case."

"That is good!" Mantu said, his smile broadening still more and his coal-black eyes glistening. "Now we have much work to do."

Aside from the photograph of Niki, which wasn't much to go on since it was taken years before, the African told them about another point of identification; one they wouldn't mistake.

Niki Jerusa was missing the little finger on her left hand!

"I believe she lost it on the night of the revolt. You should have no trouble making a positive identification if you find her," Mantu explained.

"So where do we begin looking?" Frank asked.

Mantu took out a pad and started jotting down words. "A beautician on the Left Bank of Paris," he said. "Here is her name and the address of the beauty salon where she works."

"Fine," Frank said, taking the address as well as a credit card they were to use for expenses. "When do we leave?"

"Now. Your flight takes off in two hours."

"Two hours!?"

Mantu laughed and his black eyes blazed. "Yes. I will be flying back to Zebwa on another plane at the same time. Now go pack. Be quick."

Frank and Joe ran upstairs, threw clothes in suitcases, hugged Laura Hardy good-bye, called their father in New York, and were on their way to the airport within an hour.

"You are to contact me through your home if you locate Niki," Mantu told them at the airport terminal while handing out their tickets. "Do you have any more questions?"

Frank shook his head to the negative, at the same time glancing over the African's shoulder. A man in a beige raincoat stood in the corner of the waiting room reading a newspaper. Frank had noticed the man lurking nearby at other spots in the airport and was beginning to wonder if they were being tailed.

"Then I wish you luck for the sake of Zebwa," Mantu said and smiled in parting. "Remember, the future of our nation may well depend on you. Good-bye, my young friends."

With a clipped but dramatic bow, the man from Zebwa then disappeared into the crowd to board his own flight to Africa. Minutes later, the Hardys were

24

taking seats on a Boeing 747 jetliner bound for Paris, France.

The man in the beige raincoat also boarded.

"Don't stare, but I think we've got company," Frank whispered, once the jet had broken through the clouds at twenty thousand feet. "Check out that guy two rows back."

Joe purposely dropped a magazine, glancing back as he retrieved it. With a puffy, babyish face and an unusually wide mouth, the strange man sat calmly reading his newspaper as if Joe's glance meant nothing to him. But the two young detectives had long ago developed a sixth sense about being followed.

"Looks like a pro," Joe whispered back, resuming his upright position. "You want to try talking to him?"

"No. I'm sure he has a pat story and would stick with it. Let's just ditch him when we land."

Joe nodded, then looked questioningly at his brother, who was gazing thoughtfully out the window at the ocean below.

"You got any theories?"

"He might be working for the Tota rebels," Frank spoke in a hushed tone.

Joe grimaced. "I bet you're right. They'd have every reason to want to prevent Niki from returning to Zebwa."

The boys knew that preventing Niki from returning to Zebwa could well mean taking her life. If the Tota rebels were as cruel as they were reputed to be, they'd go to any lengths to make sure that Jerusa loyalists didn't bring Niki back to rally the people's support. It was very possible they'd learned of Mantu's quest for her and had been following him all along.

"And now he's following us." The blond boy frowned.

"Exactly. Which means we gotta lose him before we get anywhere near Niki."

Joe nodded, barely able to restrain himself from taking another look at the strange man behind them. "I wonder if he's the same guy who broke in last night."

"Me, too. Maybe he was just spying on us so he could make sure we were taking the case. That would explain his eavesdropping on our conversation with Dad. Whether he was or not, though, let's lose him in Paris. And pronto."

The weather was warm and sunny at DeGaulle International when the 747 finally touched down eight hours later. The Hardys left the airport terminal, hailed a taxi, and headed straight for downtown Paris, where they began a series of maneuvers within the city's extensive underground Metro system—hopping subway cars, doubling back, and at last hiding among some empty fruit crates at a

Metro station until they were sure the baby-faced man in the raincoat had been shaken.

"Well, that takes care of him," Joe said with a grin as they exited the Metro at Boulevard St. Jacques.

The busy, cafe-lined street was in an area of Paris known as the Left Bank, or Latin Quarter, where artists, students, and political radicals flocked from all over the globe. It was also where Mantu believed they would find Niki Jerusa. A uniformed gendarme directed the boys up a narrow side street to the address Mantu had given them. It was a New Wave beauty salon, specializing in punk hairdos.

"*Oui*, I believe that is her," the beautician informed them, taking the time to look at Niki's picture when she had finished dyeing one teenager's hair orange and green and cutting it into a kind of Mohawk with spikes. "Her name is Michelle. But she has not come here for a long time. She was a very wild and rootless girl, this Michelle."

"Do you remember if she was missing the little finger on her left hand?" Frank queried, figuring Niki may well have changed her name to avoid detection.

"I do not know. She wore a shiny silver glove on her left hand. Maybe she was missing the little finger or maybe no."

Many of the salon patrons were dressed as bizarrely as their hairstyles. For Niki to adopt the punked-out look would be a perfect way to excuse

27

hiding her missing finger with a single glove on her left hand.

"Did Niki, I mean Michelle, ever talk about where she was living?" Joe asked.

"She did not say. All I know is that she was a waitress at some nightclub."

"Did she tell you which nightclub?"

The hairstylist shook her head thoughtfully. "No, but I remember she spoke to me one time about a special dessert the nightclub served. It was a kind of kiwi fruit pie."

Frank urged the woman to remember all she could about the special dessert, then used the salon pay phone, returning a few minutes later grinning from ear to ear. "I called a Paris restaurant critic. He said the only nightclub with a kiwi fruit pie is the Lapin Noir. It's not far from here."

"Then what are we waiting for!" Joe beamed, starting out the door.

"Please wait!" the beautician called, stopping the boys. "If you would like to find this Michelle, she is easy to tell because of her hair."

"Her hair?" Frank asked.

"Yes, her hair! It is purple!"

Hurrying from the salon, the boys crossed a bridge spanning the Seine River and found the Lapin Noir nightclub. But their hopes soon crumbled. Nobody even vaguely resembling Niki worked in the club, much less someone with so outstanding a feature as purple hair! The restaurant manager informed them that Michelle had indeed waitressed there several months before, but he had no clue where she was now. All he could give them was her former address.

"I should've known it wouldn't be this easy," Joe shrugged as they left the nightclub. "I guess we might as well check out Niki's old address. Maybe the landlord or a neighbor will have some idea where she is."

Frank suddenly froze and grabbed Joe's arm. "I don't believe it!" he uttered, fixing his eyes on the far side of the street.

Joe's jaw dropped as he followed his brother's gaze. It was the mysterious baby-faced man who had tailed them all the way from Bayport. He was leaning against a lamppost, casually reading his newspaper.

"How did he find us?!" Joe cried in disbelief.

Frank growled under his breath. "Let's ask him."

Seeing the boys start for him, the man quickly folded his paper and began to trot toward a set of stairs leading underground.

"He's heading for the Metro!" Frank shouted, breaking into a run.

The brothers were halfway across the street and the baby-faced man was beginning to descend the Metro stairway when a voice suddenly cried out from behind them.

"Stop! I know where Michelle is!"

3 Flying French Fists

The brothers looked back to see a figure beckoning them from an alley next to the Lapin Noir. The fading sunlight made him hard to distinguish at first, but in a moment they recognized him as the nightclub's bartender.

"Come here! It is about Michelle!" the bartender shouted from the alley, waving frantically. He had a full mustache, sideburns, and a flowered shirt unbuttoned down to the middle of his chest.

Frank looked back across the street for the man in the raincoat, who had already disappeared down the crowded Metro station stairway.

"Let's drop him for now," he said, deciding it was more important to locate Niki quickly than to waste time chasing the man.

Joining the bartender in the alley, the sleuths saw he was not much older than they and only looked it because of the sideburns and mustache.

"Hello, I am Phillipe," he said excitedly. "I heard you ask the manager about Michelle. I know where you can find her."

"Okay, fine," Frank said. "But why couldn't you have told us when we were inside?"

"Follow me. I will show you."

Frank and Joe were led down the alley to another one running behind the Lapin Noir nightclub. Upon turning the corner, they stopped in their tracks.

Six nightclub waiters stood in a row—their jackets off and sleeves rolled up for battle!

The Hardys started to back off, but it was too late. Phillipe grabbed Joe from behind and held him as a muscular waiter stepped up and planted his fist on the blond detective's lip.

At the same time, the other five surrounded Frank.

"What's the big idea?" Joe snapped, struggling to free himself from the bartender's grasp.

"The big idea?" the bartender hissed over Joe's shoulder. "The big idea is to give you punks a taste of what happens to nosy guys who ask too many questions."

Joe could taste it all right. The salty flavor of blood filled his mouth as a second blow struck the other side of his face.

"But we were only . . ."

The young detective saw his attacker wind up for a stomach punch and was suddenly in no mood to do any more arguing in French. There was only one language being spoken right now. He coiled his leg, directing his heel in a karate kick straight to the waiter's solar plexus.

"*Ummmmpphhh!*"

The muscular waiter's knees buckled and he crumpled to the brick pavement, gasping for breath. In the same second, Joe wrested his arms from Phillipe and dropped him with a lightning right hook to the jaw.

Outnumbered four to one and sporting a bloody nose, Frank was having a little more trouble freeing himself. Joe dove into the crowd, landing a flying tackle on one and toppling two others like dominoes.

"Let's get out of here!" Frank cried, leaving the last one dazed with a combination punch to the ribs and face.

Before the bartender and his gang of waiters had time to recover, the brothers ran down the alley and out into the street, not stopping to rest until they were in a public park several blocks away.

"Well, what do you think of gay Paree now?" Frank grinned, lying on a park bench with his head tilted back to stop the flow of blood from his nose.

Joe laughed as he mopped his lip with a tissue. "It reminds me of home."

The older boy smiled, remembering all the times they'd fought and beaten the odds back in their home town of Bayport. Then he sighed. "Well, it wasn't the easiest way to get information, but it's obvious Phillipe knows Niki and probably where she's living."

"Then let's go rent ourselves a couple of Mopeds."

Mopeds is a brand of motorbike common to Parisian streets, and the brothers had noticed a group of them lined up in the alley behind the Lapin Noir, probably belonging to the bartender and his gang of waiters. With two of their own, Frank and Joe would be able to tail the bartender once he got off work. If they were lucky, he'd lead them straight to Niki.

Using the credit card Mantu had given them, the boys rented Mopeds at a motorbike shop, then stationed themselves outside the Lapin Noire. They scouted the area and found no trace of the man in the raincoat, so they trusted they weren't in any danger of being followed themselves.

At ten past midnight, the nightclub employees finally poured out of the alley from behind the Lapin Noire and buzzed down the street on their Mopeds. Some broke off in different directions, but others stayed in a pack with the mustached bartender, including the one who'd bullied Joe.

"Let's keep our distance," Frank said, releasing his Moped's kick stand. "They might suspect this."

A warm summer breeze, mixed with the aromas of freshly baked bread, sweet French pastries, and exotic sauces, filled the glittering, cafe-lined streets of Paris as the brothers chugged along on their Mopeds. Even after midnight, the city brimmed with activity, and it was hard for them to keep a clear view of Phillipe's bike and yet stay at a safe distance.

"This sure is a good place to get lost in, if you're looking to get lost," Frank declared as they passed the Louvre Museum and crossed the dark Seine River again.

"I know," Joe said distractedly. He was gazing out on the endless universe of twinkling lights called Paris. Somewhere among them was the little girl in the photo, now older, orphaned, and exiled from her native land. Somewhere out there was also a man in a raincoat who may well have been hired to kill her.

"I hope we're doing the right thing," he said.

"Me, too. Whatever we think of his methods, Phillipe's sure doing his best to protect Niki."

The pack of Mopeds suddenly made a sharp right turn onto a narrow street and the Hardys raced their engines a little to pick up the slack. As they

34

did, they saw the bartender and his friends come to a stop at a small cafe halfway up the block.

Phillipe had dismounted his motorbike and was hugging a slender girl with bright purple hair!

"That's her!" Joe cried out without thinking. "It's Niki!"

Unluckily, Joe's exclamation caught the bartender's attention.

"Nice play, Shakespeare," Frank muttered, spinning his Moped around. "Let's take off. One beating a day is enough for me."

In seconds, Phillipe's gang was back on their bikes in pursuit. And by the time the sleuths were at the corner again, the gang was only thirty yards back and gaining fast.

Frank's eyes suddenly grew wide. "Where did *he* come from?!" he cried.

It was the baby-faced man, rounding the corner on foot just as the sleuths took the same corner going in the opposite direction. Without so much as a glance at the boys, the man marched briskly up the sidewalk—straight for the cafe and Niki!

Joe's pulse quickened and he felt his mouth go dry. "I don't know how, but we've gotta get back to Niki fast!"

Both boys looked back and saw the bartender's gang swarm down the street and zoom right by the baby-faced man. Niki now stood unprotected and alone at the cafe door.

"That's great!" Frank groaned sarcastically. "She's a sitting duck!"

"We can't just leave her!" Joe nearly screamed.

"Of course not! Turn right!"

The boys knew it would be pointless to stop and explain the situation to Phillipe and his gang. Their only hope was to somehow evade the gang and get back to the cafe before the baby-faced man could do any damage. The chance of that looked slim, but it was worth a try. With the gang less than a few bike lengths behind, Frank and Joe made a screeching right turn up the next block under full throttle. But their bikes weren't as well tuned as their pursuers' were, and by the time they were halfway around the block, Phillipe had overtaken them and was in the process of maneuvering to cut Joe off.

"Watch out!" Frank shouted.

Joe, having been preoccupied with two bikes closing in from the rear, shifted focus to his left just in time to see the mustached French youth veer sharply in an attempt to run him into a wall of parked cars. Joe swerved just in time to avoid a full broadside as Phillipe's front tire grazed his back tire and, after a few wobbly seconds, he managed to regain control and steer clear of the parked cars. He then looked back to see Phillipe moving up for another strike.

In the meantime, Frank had jumped the curb and

was speeding along the sidewalk using the barrier of parked cars as a shield. Three of the waiters were keeping pace with him out on the street, though, preparing to intercept him when the line of cars ended at the corner.

Then a milk truck turned up the street.

This was just the break Joe needed. He dodged in front of the truck, causing it to screech to a stop right in front of his pursuers.

CRASH!!

In a fruitless skid to avoid the milk truck, the gang's Mopeds flew out from under them and slammed into the vehicle. Phillipe's bike spun around on its side several times before wedging itself under the truck's front fender.

Hearing the smash-up, Frank took advantage of the confusion by shooting out from between two parked cars and jumping the curb on the far side of the street. From there, he flew up into the courtyard of an old apartment building. By the time he'd spun around the courtyard fountain and plowed through a hedge of bushes, the remaining gang members were too busy falling over each other to keep up the chase.

While Phillipe struggled to extract his Moped from under the milk truck and the truck driver cursed in French, Frank and Joe joined up at the end of the block and looped back to the street where the cafe was. They turned the corner just in time to witness the man in the raincoat grab Niki!

"He's got her!" Joe exclaimed, fearing they were too late.

The purple-haired girl struggled in the man's grasp, looking as helpless as a fly in a spider's web.

"HELP ME!!"

4 The Queen

"Let go of her!" Frank yelled angrily.

This time the baby-faced stranger in the raincoat glanced up at the brothers, but he didn't let go. He had grabbed the girl's left arm and was trying to yank her silver-sparkled glove off as she flailed at him with her free hand. Without flinching, the man continued ripping at the glove, getting it off just as Frank and Joe reached the cafe.

"I said let go of her!" Frank shouted again, stopping at the curb and pushing aside cafe tables.

Suddenly, the man did let go, but not because of Frank's warning. He quickly threw the glove to the ground and backed off, leaving the girl confused and in tears.

"Okay, buddy!" Joe spat, clenching his fists. "You're history!"

The blond boy took two steps forward, then stopped in his tracks as the man pulled a .38-caliber automatic from his jacket!

"Don't make me use this," he spoke calmly, leveling the gun at the brothers and backing down the sidewalk. "I don't want to hurt anyone."

His tone left no doubt that, while he really didn't want to, he'd use the gun without a moment's hesitation if necessary. The Hardys froze, lifting their palms over their heads in a gesture of surrender.

"But why have you been following us?" Frank asked gingerly. "And what do you want with Niki?"

The stranger didn't reply. He just kept walking backwards until he was at a safe distance, then he disappeared around the corner. When he was out of sight, Frank and Joe at last focused their attention on his victim.

"Thank you so much," the purple-haired girl breathed. "I thought he was going to kill me." Her face was streaked with tears and she massaged her left wrist, having hurt it in the tussle over the glove.

"So did we, Niki," Frank sighed. "And I'm afraid we're the ones who led him to you. But don't worry, Niki, you're safe. . . ."

"Niki? Niki!?" the girl suddenly cried, almost

hysterically. "Why does everyone think my name is Niki? I am Michelle!"

"Come on, Niki," Joe said with a smile. "You don't have to fake it with us. We've come to help you return to Zebwa. . . ."

As Joe spoke, his eyes wandered down to the girl's left hand, which she was still holding and massaging. All her fingers were there, including her pinky! She couldn't be Niki Jerusa!

"You aren't Niki at all!" he exclaimed, his mouth dropping in surprise.

"That's what I keep trying to tell you! I am Michelle! That man thought my name was Niki, and now you call me Niki! What is going on here?"

The two brothers exchanged incredulous looks, realizing why the man in the raincoat had suddenly lost interest in the girl.

"Gee, we're sorry," Frank said, redfaced. "We really thought you were someone else."

Frank then heard the whine of Moped engines approaching from the rear, and he turned to see the bartender's gang on their way down the street.

"Uh-oh! Here they come again!"

Suddenly, the girl seemed to come to a realization of her own. "You mean you were the two boys they were chasing?" she asked.

"That's us," Joe gulped, seeing it was too late to do anything other than try and defend themselves as best they could.

41

"Then my parents didn't send you to look for me?" the girl persisted.

Phillipe and the waiters climbed off their motorbikes. They were bruised and angry over their collision with the milk truck, and they marched toward the Hardys, determined to beat the daylights out of them.

Frank positioned himself behind a table. "Look, Michelle, we don't know anything about your parents. But we sure would appreciate it if you'd call off your boyfriend before this gets out of hand."

"Phillipe! Phillipe! Stop!" the girl cried, running up to the bartender. "They were looking for some other girl who they thought was me. My parents did not send them!"

The bartender paused, as if considering whether to go ahead with the beating anyway, after all the trouble the Hardys had put them through. He glared at Frank and Joe, then his eyes grew soft as he looked lovingly at Michelle.

"Are you sure, honey?" he asked. "They might be lying, you know."

"They say they mistook me for some girl called Niki," Michelle explained.

The nightclub employee frowned. "Then why didn't they ask about this Niki instead of you? I think they are lying."

He started toward the brothers again, the waiters eagerly ready to back him up.

"Wait," Frank spoke in a calm voice. "I'll tell you what. Let us explain, and if you aren't satisfied with what we have to say, you can do what you want with us. Okay? We'll even let you tie us up if you'd like."

Phillipe stopped again. If Michelle hadn't been there, he wouldn't have listened to Frank for one second before clobbering him. But to go on with the beating now would just make him look like a brutal bully.

"Okay," he snarled. "We tie you up and you talk."

The Hardys were roughly strapped to cafe chairs, their waists bound by steel cables which the waiters usually used to lock their Mopeds. Then Frank showed them the old photo of Niki, which bore a strong resemblance to Michelle, and explained their reasons for believing she'd changed her name to hide her identity.

"We're sorry," Joe concluded for his brother. "But there were just too many coincidences. Both girls look the same, both are from Africa, both are about the same age. And Michelle is on the run just as Niki's supposed to be. All that plus the glove, which we believed was to conceal proof of the missing finger, made us certain Michelle was really Niki Jerusa."

"That is so exciting!" Michelle beamed, clapping her hands. "As you say, I am from Africa, too. I know all about the trouble in Zebwa. I even remember seeing pictures of this Niki Jerusa in the newspaper after the revolution. Do you think you can find her?"

"It doesn't look good," Frank sighed, finally being released from the chair. "Now we don't have any idea where she might be. It could be anywhere in the world for all we know."

Frank then turned his gaze on the purple-haired girl. "What about *you?* You mentioned something about your parents?"

A deep sadness came over Michelle's face, only to be replaced by a sudden flash of anger. "Yes, my parents," she answered bitterly. "I ran away from the boarding school they sent me to. Now they are trying to find me to send me back."

"And you don't want to go back," the young detective led her on, keenly interested in the story that had cost them bloody lips and noses earlier that day.

Michelle shook her head emotionally. "I hated it. And I hate my parents. They made me go there when I was only six years old because I was just a nuisance to them. They are rich and spend all of their time traveling with the jet set all over the world, so they have no time for raising me. The boarding school is just an excuse so they won't feel guilty about abandoning me. Oh, I hate them so much! They rejected me and now I reject them!"

"You think they've hired someone to find you?" Frank asked sympathetically.

"Yes. That's why I change my jobs and addresses all the time. And that's why I ask Phillipe to keep anybody from finding where I am. My mother and father just want me back in school so they won't have to worry about me and can go on with their fancy lives. I hate them, I hate school, and I am not going back there ever again!"

"Hello, Michelle," a gentle female voice spoke up out of the darkness.

The Hardys saw Michelle's face harden like a rock, and they looked back to see a nicely dressed woman in her forties standing on the sidewalk. Tears were in her eyes and her face was formed in a tentative smile as she nervously clutched her handbag.

"Hello, Mama," Michelle responded, her tone cold and her eyes fixed in an icy stare.

The young runaway then shot an accusing look at Frank and Joe, and Phillipe angrily grabbed Joe by his shirt collar.

"I knew you punks were liars!" he snapped. "You led her here, didn't you?"

"They did not lead me anywhere," the woman said, still gazing with misty eyes upon her purple-haired daughter. "I found her myself."

Phillipe let go of Joe's shirt as the woman timidly approached Michelle.

"I've missed you, honey," she said nervously. "I've been looking for you for weeks. I know I haven't been much of a mother, and I'll understand

45

if you don't want to come home. But when you ran away from school I realized how much I really cared for you."

"You don't care about me at all," Michelle spat, still glaring at her mother.

"Yes I do," the middle-aged woman pleaded, as fresh tears began rolling down her cheeks. "I love you very much, and so does your father. We promise we'll never send you back to that school. We want you with us. I know I can't make up for all the years we missed together, but I'd like to try."

"You've been looking for me all this time all by yourself?" Michelle asked. She was trying hard to stay angry, but Frank and Joe could tell she was starting to crack around the edges.

The woman nodded, nervously fidgeting with her purse straps. "I've been all over the country, every night at a hotel in a different city, every day posting your picture on bulletin boards. I'm so glad I finally found you. I love you, honey. Though I must say," she smiled through her tears, "I don't especially love your choice of hair color."

Unable to contain herself anymore, Michelle jumped from her chair and threw her arms around her mother.

"Oh, Mama! I love you, too!"

With everyone caught up in this touching mother-and-daughter reunion, Frank and Joe slipped away on their Mopeds and cruised off down the street. It was almost three o'clock in the morning.

"Where do we go from here?" Joe sighed as they crossed over the Seine again. "Niki could be anywhere."

The French city was now mostly quiet. The midnight crowds were gone from the cafes, and only the street lamps lit the young detectives' way through the night.

"I say we check into a hotel and worry about it after we've had some sleep," Frank answered. "I'm just as glad Michelle wasn't Niki after all. Who knows what that guy would've done to her if he'd found her little finger missing."

"But how did he find us?" Joe groaned with frustration. "I thought we'd lost him twice for sure."

"I don't know." The older boy shrugged.

The brothers checked into a cheap hotel and searched their clothes for bugging devices before they crashed out for the night. They didn't find any. In the morning, they got up late and placed a transatlantic call to Bayport, leaving word that Mantu's lead had been a dead end. Mantu hadn't called the Hardy home yet himself.

"I should call Iola," Joe said once they were off the phone. "Maybe she's cooled off a little by now."

Joe dialed the Mortons' home number and got his girlfriend on the line. She was still a little sore at

47

first, but when Joe said how sorry he was and that he hoped to make amends by buying her some perfume, she softened a little.

"Forget the perfume," Iola's distant voice sighed over the line. "I'm sorry, I guess I just have some trouble handling your running off all the time on a minute's notice. When are you coming back?"

"It doesn't look like it'll be very soon," Joe replied. "And I'm sorry, too. I wish I could be there for that contest. How's it going, anyway?"

Joe didn't dare bring up the name Jim Gunther, for fear it would start an argument. But there was another reason as well—trust. He didn't want to lose Iola, but if he had to worry about her whenever he was away on a case, the relationship wasn't worth it. This would be a major test. Jim Gunther would no doubt try to make a move on Iola in Joe's absence.

"Oh, the contest's going pretty well, I guess," Iola replied. "I think I did great on the preliminaries. But the finals are tonight, and that's what really counts."

"How about the competition?"

"Not too heavy. There's this one girl who's doing better than everyone on the talent part, but I'll bet I got her beat on looks."

"How come?" Joe chuckled into the receiver. "Is she ugly?"

48

"No, she's very pretty. I think she's from Africa or something. But one of her fingers is missing. How can you expect to win a beauty contest without all your fingers?!"

Joe sat up in bed. "Which finger?"

"The little finger on her left hand. Why?"

"Because she might be the very girl we came all the way to Paris to look for!" the blond boy exclaimed into the receiver. "Do you know her name?"

"I think it's Mickey or something. Does this mean you'll be coming back for the finals this afternoon?"

"We're sure gonna try!"

Joe hung the phone up and snapped his fingers with glee. "She's been in Bayport all along! We've got to catch the first plane back home!"

The sleuths threw their things back in their suitcases, caught a cab to the airport, and boarded the first jet back to the States. The flight seemed to last forever, and by the time they had landed, the contest was already well underway. They hopped another cab and were driven straight to the auditorium where it was being held.

"There she is!" Joe cried out as they entered the building in time to see Miss Barmet Bay be crowned.

The new beauty queen was indeed Niki Jerusa. There was no mistake about it this time. She stood center stage as the crown was placed on her head. Iola, in her yellow satin gown, was on Niki's right, having taken second place.

"And there's Mantu!" Frank uttered, spotting the tall African with the coal-black eyes in the crowd.

5 Niki's Story

"What's he doing here?" Joe wondered aloud. "He's supposed to be in Africa."

"Good question," Frank said, knitting his brow.

Mantu was at the front of the crowd, watching Niki as she accepted a bouquet of roses and blew a farewell kiss to the audience. The teenaged African girl was even more stunning than they'd imagined.

"Shall we talk to him or Niki first?" Joe asked, when the beauty contestants finally filed off the stage.

"Niki," Frank replied tersely. "See if you can get Iola to let us go backstage."

Frank and Joe went to the entrance of the

dressing-room area and asked to see Iola. A moment later, she appeared in her yellow satin gown.

"Hi," Joe said quickly. "We have to see the girl who won. Can you get us backstage? It's important."

"Sure. She's in dressing room nine," the pretty high-school junior spoke, then put her hands on her hips in disgust. "Aren't you even going to congratulate me?"

"Oh, yeah. Congratulations," Joe replied, carelessly brushing by his girlfriend in a hurry to get to Niki before Mantu did.

"What about my perfume!"

"Sorry! Didn't have time!" Joe called back as he ran down the hall.

"Thanks a lot!" Iola muttered sarcastically to herself, now more miffed than ever. Her eyes then focused on Jim Gunther, who stood in front of her with an eager smile and a bouquet of daisies.

"These are for you," he said, handing her the flowers. "And I thought you were the winner by a mile."

"Thanks," the strawberry blonde smiled back. "I'm glad *somebody* feels that way."

Frank and Joe found dressing room nine and knocked on the door. In a moment, Niki opened it still dressed in her pageant gown.

"You're Niki Jerusa, aren't you?" Frank asked.

The beauty queen's eyes became wary. "Maybe."

"We're friends," Frank assured her. "We don't have time to explain right now, but please do us a favor and lock yourself inside your room for a few minutes. Your safety may be at stake."

Suddenly a look of dread covered the girl's face. "Is it someone from Zebwa?"

"Yes. But if you stay in there and keep your door locked, you won't be in any danger. We'll be back in a couple of minutes."

With a frightened nod, Niki shut the door and the Hardys heard the sound of it being bolted. Then the boys ran back down the hall and intercepted Mantu, who had also managed to gain backstage entry somehow. He was more surprised to see them than they were to see him.

"What are you doing here?" he demanded.

Joe explained their lucky discovery and how they'd just flown back from Paris, then he turned his suspicions on Mantu.

"You said you were going back to Africa."

"Oh, yes." The tall man grinned. "I was going to go back. But at the airport I happened to pick up a newspaper with an article about the beauty contest. There was a picture in it of all the girls, and one of them looked so much like Niki that I decided to cancel my flight. You see?"

Frank studied the man closely, trying to read his reactions. "We just told Niki to lock herself in her dressing room," he spoke evenly. "She knows she's being hunted, and she was scared to death to learn that someone from Zebwa was looking for her."

"She has nothing to fear from me," Mantu defended himself, his black eyes betraying nothing. "I will go and see her now."

"Not until we're sure it's okay with her," Joe said firmly, stepping directly in front of the African.

Mantu's eyes showed intense anger for an instant, since the boys he'd hired to find Niki were now preventing him from seeing her. Then he seemed to calm down a little. "Fine," he said nervously. "You go tell her I want to talk to her."

"We have to get a few things straight first," Frank told him.

"Okay, what things?" Mantu frowned, leaning up against the hall wall.

Frank explained about the mysterious man who had followed them to Paris, apparently after Niki. "It's not that we doubt you. It's just that we have to be very careful. Niki's life may be at stake and we don't want to let anyone get near her unless it's okay with her. Understand?"

Mantu nodded. "Yes, I understand now why you are so cautious. And you are right. The man who followed you was one of the rebels. His job is to kill her. I guess he followed me, too, and I never knew it. But now it is more important than ever that she return to the safety of her own people. Do you understand *that?*"

"What matters is that Niki understands," Joe responded. "You wait here."

As Mantu stood anxiously in the backstage hallway, the brothers returned to Niki's dressing room. Niki opened the door a crack to make sure it was them, then let them in, locking the door again once they were inside.

"I know who Mantu is," she said when they'd finished describing him. "He was a corporal in my father's army."

"Then there's no chance he's one of the Tota rebels?" Joe queried.

"No. But it isn't only the Totas I'm afraid of," the pretty young African told them, her voice full of emotion. "There was a traitor among my father's own men. A traitor who may well want to see me dead."

The brothers looked at each other in amazement.

"What do you mean?" Frank asked, gazing in wonder at the distraught beauty queen.

"You see," Niki began, then stopped speaking for a moment. Uneasy about the subject, she started to pace back and forth in her dressing room. "The rebel revolt was only part of the reason I fled Zebwa and went into hiding. I also witnessed my father's assassination, and it was by one of his own men."

"His own men?"

"Yes. And I was the only witness. The traitor thinks I am the only one who can identify him, and he would surely try to kill me if I were to return to Zebwa."

"So you know who the traitor is?" Frank asked, confused that she hadn't identified her father's assassin long ago.

Niki threw her hands in the air. "I have no idea who he is! I only know he is someone high up in my father's government."

"But you said you witnessed—" Joe began.

"I did!" Niki exclaimed. "But he was wearing a tribal mask and the room was very dark, so it could have been any one of a lot of people!"

"You'd better just tell your story from the beginning," Frank said calmly, now more confused than ever.

Niki Jerusa sat down for a moment until she was collected enough to tell her tale. On the night of the revolution, she had gone to her father's bedroom in the presidential palace to say good night. Upon entering, she saw a man standing over her father's body with a knife in his hand and an African tribal mask on his face. The man had then fled the scene without Niki ever discovering his identity, only that it had to be someone her father trusted enough to let in his heavily guarded palace at night, as well as someone who had reason to conceal his identity— such as a high official in the Jerusa government. Within hours after news of the assassination, the palace was stormed by heavily armed Tota rebels and all those inside had either been killed or had escaped into the jungle.

"So you see why I could never return to Zebwa," Niki explained. "Any one of my father's men could have been the killer. Even Mantu himself, though I doubt he was high-ranking enough to enter the palace at night. My father's security was very tight."

"And you've been afraid all this time that your father's assassin would track you down and kill you too," Joe said sympathetically.

"He might think I recognized him even with his mask on," she nodded. "I would then be the only witness."

Frank looked curiously at the girl. "If you don't mind my asking, why did you enter a beauty contest if you were so desperate to hide? Wasn't that a little risky with all the publicity?"

Niki sighed. "I'm tired of running," she said simply. "I have to go on with my life."

"Would that mean returning to Zebwa and helping your people if you had the chance?" Joe queried.

"Yes, I'd like that more than anything. But I'm afraid that that is impossible with my father's killer loose."

Frank and Joe could see that Niki had matured since fleeing her country. Her desperate life since the revolution had forced her to grow up quickly. Now all Niki Jerusa wanted was to go back home, happy to lead her people in their cause if it weren't for the fact that there was a murderous traitor among them.

"Wait here," Frank said, standing up. "We'll see what Mantu has to say about all this."

Frank and Joe left Niki's dressing room again and met Mantu in the hall. They told him Niki's fears and explained why it was unsafe for her to return to Zebwa.

"I never knew she had seen the assassination," Mantu told them, knitting his brow. "The poor girl. I understand how she feels. But we caught the traitor and had him executed for his crime last year. He was one of President Jerusa's most trusted cabinet ministers—a man named Bidoli. We think the rebels made a deal with him. It is sad, but Niki has nothing to fear from her father's assassin. Bidoli is long dead."

Mantu's story seemed to jive with the research the brothers had done on the Zebwa revolution, but before returning to Niki they wanted to double-check it with their father's operative. They called Sam Radley from a pay phone and had Mantu's story confirmed. A man named Bidoli had indeed apparently been the traitor and was executed by the Jerusa loyalists after the revolt. Mantu seemed to be on the level.

"Thanks, Sam," Joe said. He hung up the phone and then turned to Frank. "It all checks out. Let's tell Niki."

The pageant winner had mixed emotions about the news. Bidoli had been like an uncle to her, and to think that he'd killed her father deeply saddened her. But at the same time, this meant she now would be able to return to her home country and help her father's supporters regain power from the rebels.

"I will talk to Mantu now," she said with determination.

"What about the scholarship you got for winning the contest?" Joe kidded her as they left the dressing room.

"Oh, I'll give that to the second-place girl. She seemed very nice."

Joe grinned, realizing this meant Iola. He could hardly wait to tell her the news.

The Hardys unlocked the dressing-room door and let Mantu in. He greeted Niki warmly and assured her again and again that she had nothing to fear.

"We will go back to Zebwa tonight." He smiled. "It is urgent that we move quickly, for the sake of our people."

"I'll have to tell my aunt and uncle," Niki said, referring to her two distant relatives who lived near Bayport and had taken her in during the past year. "I'll miss them."

She then looked at Frank and Joe. "I wish you could come with us to Africa. I'd feel safer having you around. But I guess your job ends here, doesn't it?"

"Yup, sorry." Joe shrugged. "I wish we could go, too."

Mantu went to the phone and had the local operator patch him into a special overseas satellite, which relayed his signal to a radio receiver at the loyalists' encampment in Zebwa. Soon he was reporting the good news to Akutu, the former Jerusa general now in command of the loyalists' forces.

"Akutu wants to speak with you," the tall African said, handing the phone over to Frank after a few minutes.

Frank took the receiver. "Hello?"

"Congratulations on your fine work," a deep, heavily accented voice spoke distantly over the line. "You and your brother have helped us greatly, if not to find Niki, then in keeping the rebel spy away. I thank you."

"You're welcome," Frank replied, sensing that the former Jerusa general had more on his mind than congratulations.

"I have been talking to Mantu, and he says that Niki would like you to escort her here," the commander continued. "I want her to feel safe, so I would be very grateful if you would. I will not lie to you. It will be dangerous. You must take her through the rebel lines and bring her to my hidden encampment in the mountains. The rebels will do all they can to stop you, and I will understand if you decide not to accept."

"I'd like to talk it over with my brother for a

60

minute," Frank said, feeling uncomfortable with the idea.

"Of course," Akutu replied. "But you would be doing us a great service if you said yes."

Frank turned to discuss Akutu's proposal with Joe. In addition to Niki's own eagerness to have them as an escort, they had begun to feel responsible for the girl's safety. To abandon her now wouldn't sit well on their consciences.

"We'll do it," Frank said into the phone.

"You are brave lads and I am honored," the deep voice replied. "Mantu will give you all your instructions."

Frank handed the phone back over to Mantu, who began to jot down information.

"I'm so happy you're coming!" Niki said gleefully.

"And we're happy that you're happy." Joe smiled, despite the fact that, inside, he felt a little queasy.

Once Mantu was off the phone, he turned to the Hardys. "We are to leave tonight. Can you be ready?"

"Why not?" Frank laughed, getting used to the African's habit of giving very short notice. "Let's go!"

The foursome left the dressing room. Joe scanned the auditorium for Iola to give her the good news about the scholarship, but all he could find was her overweight brother, Chet Morton. Chet was the brothers' best friend and had often helped them unravel mysteries.

"Oh, she took off with Jim Gunther," Chet told him. "What are you guys up to, anyway?"

Dismayed that Iola hadn't waited for him, Joe followed Mantu out of the building and filled Chet in on their mission.

"Wow! Africa!" the plump boy exclaimed. "What a gas! I wish I could go, too."

"No you don't," Joe chuckled. "It'll be pretty dangerous from what I'm told. I'm not even looking forward to it. We're just going for Niki's sake."

"I thrive on danger!" Chet asserted, puffing out his chest.

Joe laughed again. "I'll tell you what you can do, though. Go to our house and get some of our more rugged clothes. We only have the stuff we took to Paris. Then meet us at the Air Afrique terminal at the airport. Okay?"

"Aye aye, sir." Chet saluted.

Chet headed for his own car as the Hardys walked with Niki and Mantu toward his gray sedan.

"I don't believe it!" Frank gasped under his breath, spotting a figure lurking in a dark corner of the parking lot. "There he is again!"

It was the rebel spy!

Mantu quickly handed his car keys, a set of plane tickets, and a folded sheet of paper to Frank. "You take these and go to the airport. My car is rented and you can return it there. If I can't make it in time, go ahead without me and follow the instructions I have written down. Now go!"

With that, the tall African broke into a run straight for the baby-faced man, who ducked into the bushes. Soon both men were out of sight.

"Okay, let's beat it!" Joe ordered, again having forgotten all about his girlfriend—who was now out on the town with Jim Gunther.

6 Desert Passage

The young people piled into the rented car and Frank took the wheel. He drove out of the parking lot while Joe, who sat beside him, went over Mantu's instructions.

"Who was that man?" Niki asked anxiously from the back seat.

"We think he was hired by the Tota rebels," Frank told her. "With him around, it's probably best that you're leaving for Africa tonight. He was after you."

"Oh," Niki choked out in response.

Frank glanced in the rearview mirror and saw the

pretty African girl huddled in the corner, her face blank with shock.

"You don't have to do this, you know. We'd be happy to help you find a new place to hide out."

"No. I must go," Niki whispered. "My country needs me."

They stopped on the way just long enough for Niki to pack her things and say good-bye to her relatives. The young people arrived at the terminal by eight o'clock, twenty minutes before they were scheduled to take off.

"Hey, I thought you guys weren't going to make it!" Chet hailed them from the ticket counter. He was waiting with not two, but three suitcases. "I decided to come, after all," he explained. "Is it all right? My folks said I could."

Joe scanned the terminal for Mantu, but the African was nowhere in sight.

"I suppose so," Joe said. "But don't blame us if you find yourself in over your head."

"I won't," Chet promised.

Both Hardys felt uneasy about taking such liberties with Mantu's money, but since the African wasn't around to ask, they had to make the decision for him. And having Chet along seemed worth the expense.

Mantu still had not arrived when they boarded their flight to New York.

Two hours later they had caught a connecting plane to Nairobi and were soaring over the Atlantic

Ocean, for Frank and Joe the third time in almost as many days. And Nairobi would only be the second stop before a much tougher trek deep into the heart of central Africa.

Waking from a cramped night's sleep on the airliner, Frank stretched his legs and gazed out his window. In the distance, the snow-capped peak of Mount Kilimanjaro rose majestically from the grassy plains.

"Okay, guys. Rise and shine," he said, playfully poking Joe and Chet, who were sitting on either side of him. "We're almost there."

His companions groaned and opened their eyes. Niki, however, was wide awake. She had slept only fitfully and her pupils were rimmed with redness as she stared out the window at the huge mountain.

"We can still turn back," Frank said softly.

"*You* can." The girl smiled faintly. "I can't."

After landing in Kenya, the foursome chartered an old single-engine prop plane, which flew them inland to a smaller city in the desert. From there, they rented a four-wheel-drive Landrover and drove south.

"Mantu's instructions say to go straight down this road for two hundred miles," Joe stated, riding shotgun. "We should come to a town near some hills, where we're supposed to meet up with a guy named Charlie."

The road through the desert was no more than

two tire ruts in the dirt, and the Landrover left a billowing cloud of dust in its wake as it traversed the parched countryside. Niki explained that it was drought season. The droughts had grown more severe over the last few years, leaving many desert tribes unable to grow crops, and on the brink of starvation.

"Is this what Zebwa is like?" Joe asked.

"Half of it," the African girl replied. "There's a mountain range running through the middle of the country. On one side there is jungle, and the other side is desert like this."

Joe squinted toward the horizon, where he could make out several mountains in the distance. The few trees and bushes which dotted the dirt road were withered and brown, and under the noon sun the temperature had climbed to a scorching 102°. Luckily, the young people had brought plenty of water along for the trip, and they took frequent sips from canteens to wash the heat and dust from their throats.

"Hey, look! A tribal village!" Chet exclaimed. "Where's my camera?"

A line of mud huts with thatched roofs appeared, and Chet eagerly cocked his camera for some shots of the colorfully costumed natives he expected to see. But when they arrived at the village, the enthusiasm drained from his face as quickly as it had come. Instead of the brightly dressed Africans, a scene of horror greeted him.

"Oh!" He shuddered, dropping the camera in his lap.

Children with blank faces and skeletal bodies came to the side of the road, their arms as thin as twigs and their stomachs distended—a sign of acute starvation. The youngsters were too weak from hunger to even hold out their little hands to beg. They just stood, staring like zombies at the Landrover.

"Stop!" Niki commanded.

Frank pulled to the side and the girl climbed out, carrying two water containers. Joe followed her with the brown paper bag full of ham sandwiches which they had made for lunch. The children were too shy to come near, but at the sight of the food and water, their parents emerged from the mud huts and gratefully accepted the offering.

"I wish we had more to give them." Niki sighed once they were back in the car. "I had no idea things were this bad."

Nobody said a word, and Chet stared forlornly. He was so ashamed of his over-ample physique amid the horrible reality of famine that he had been too embarrassed to leave the Landrover while the food was being given away.

The group passed several more villages on their way, all similar to the first one. Soon, Niki had nothing more to share and there was no reason to stop. Her conviction to help her people grew with every mile, and with it grew her courage to face the perils ahead.

"The people in my country's desert region must also be starving," she said sadly. "I am going to help them. Or I am going to die trying."

Chet gulped. All this misery was having just the opposite effect on him. He wanted out. But it was too late now.

The sun was low in the sky when they finally reached their destination, a small town at one end of the mountain range. Zebwa's borders began only a few miles away.

"That must be the place," Niki said, pointing ahead to a wood-framed house standing among a group of mud huts.

The people in the town were nearly as hungry as those in the desert villages, but the man who answered the door looked well fed. In fact, he was even rounder than Chet!

"Yes, I am Charlie!" he greeted the foursome, his belly jiggling like Santa Claus's as he laughed for no apparent reason. "I have been waiting for you! Please come in. You are just in time for dinner."

Chet all but forgot his guilt over the starving villagers and nearly pushed his way through the door, driven by his own acute hunger. He was still the same old Chet, but from this day forth he would never take a cheeseburger for granted again. Niki's response was cooler. She took an immediate dislike

69

to this man who could live so well, in the presence of such poverty, without sharing his wealth. But an ally was an ally, so she bit her lip.

"Have you heard from Mantu?" Frank asked, once they were inside the house.

Charlie shrugged. "Mantu will not be able to meet you. He is busy dealing with the rebel spy. You will be responsible for taking Niki to Akutu's camp yourself."

Frank didn't like the news and let his host know it.

"Do not worry about a thing." Charlie laughed again. "I will make sure you have a safe trip."

They all sat down at the dining-room table and were waited on by two servants who were clearly poor townsfolk. The first course was fruit salad.

"You seem to be very well off," Frank commented.

Charlie grinned impishly at the leading question. "I supply weapons to Akutu and the loyalists. They pay me well."

"Where do you get the weapons from?" Frank asked, trying to size the man up.

"Mostly the Middle Eastern countries. You see, the super powers supply many of these countries with weapons. All kinds of weapons, from jets to tanks to machine guns. But then sometimes a country will find that it has more tanks than it needs and not enough guns. That is where I come in. You could call me a kind of black-market weapons broker. If country A has too many tanks and wants more short-range cannons, and country B has too many cannons and not enough tanks, I will arrange the trade. They don't ask where I get the weapons, only that I supply them. I have even arranged such trades between countries which are actively at war with each other."

Joe leaned back, giving the man an accusing look. "Do you do the same thing with the Totas and the Jerusa loyalists, trade weapons back and forth between them without their knowing?"

"No, I don't do that," Charlie replied in a serious tone. "I am from Zebwa myself and I don't play games like that with my own people. I only supply the loyalists with weapons I acquire through my other dealings." The portly man's laugh then bubbled up again. "Don't try to be self-righteous with me, my young American friend. Many of these weapons originate from the factories in your own country."

"What about your servants?" Niki asked, changing the subject. "Do you pay *them* well?"

"They get scraps from what we don't eat . . . Ah, the main course!" he announced as one of the servants brought in a tray. "Fresh monkey!"

The servant set the steaming dish on the table. It looked like an ordinary steak covered with sauce, but even Chet suddenly lost his appetite.

"I—I guess I wasn't as hungry as I thought," he said and winced, declining the food.

71

"Oh, you must have some!" Charlie insisted, forking a large slice of the monkey steak on the boy's plate. "It is delicious! Just like hamburger!"

Chet stared at it, torn between hunger and revulsion. Not wanting to offend the man, Frank and Joe took some of the meat and nibbled on it.

Niki, though, refused it altogether.

"You will not eat?" Charlie asked her. "I would not expect this kind of squeamishness from a native African."

Niki did not answer, overcome by a sudden rush of memory. Tears were forming in her eyes, which she tried to hide but couldn't.

"I'm sorry," the pretty girl spoke at last, wiping her eyes. "I don't know what came over me."

Frank gazed sympathetically at the pretty girl. He knew that returning to Africa would be hard for her and he'd been half expecting a breakdown of this kind. After a moment of silence, she calmly explained that a monkey had saved her life the night of her father's assassination.

"A monkey saved your life?" Joe blurted.

Niki nodded. "It was a chimpanzee, actually. My father's pet. His name was Bobo."

Seeing how painful the memory was for her, Frank and Joe did not want to press her any further. But the words began to gush from Niki's lips like water from a bursting dam. For two long years she'd kept everything locked up inside, and now it was coming out at last. Almost in a trance, she recalled the events of the fateful night when her father was killed and her country overthrown.

"Bobo was in my father's chambers that evening," she began. "I didn't tell you this before, but the masked assassin didn't just run out when he saw me. He came after me with his knife. And if it hadn't been for Bobo, he would have gotten me, too."

Niki told how Bobo had leaped on top of the killer, furiously biting his hand just as she was fending off the descending blade with her own hand. In his excitement, Bobo had accidentally bitten off Niki's little finger, but he had also injured the killer enough to make him flee in pain.

"I had a ring on my finger. It was gold, with a chain of little monkeys and hippos engraved on it," Niki added, lost in the memory of the night. "My father had given it to me for my eleventh birthday."

After the incident in the bedroom, the rebels had stormed the palace. Niki had fled into the night, living like a hunted animal in the jungle for weeks before finally making it safely out of the country, never knowing who had killed her father.

"What happened to Bobo?" Frank asked gently.

"I don't know," Niki muttered, still in her trance. "I can see it so clearly. The knife coming down, its jeweled handle shining in the darkness, and Bobo landing on the man just in time to save me. I wish I did know where Bobo was. He not only saved my life, he was my closest friend. He was already with us when I was a little girl."

"You must be mistaken about the jeweled handle on the knife," Charlie spoke up with an air of superiority. "They found Bidoli's knife in your father's bedroom and determined that it was the murder weapon. It was just an ordinary knife. No jewels."

Niki sighed. "Maybe I'm wrong," she said. "It was so long ago. But I can still see it in my mind as if it were yesterday. And I remember it being jeweled. I suppose my mind is playing tricks."

"I am afraid it is," Charlie said. "It must have been a terrible shock for you."

"Did Bidoli ever confess to the assassination?" Joe asked the weapons merchant.

"I do not know," the portly man responded. "I was not there when he was caught and shot."

When the meal was over, Charlie led the foursome out to a shed in back of his house.

"Here is what you will take into Zebwa." He smiled proudly as he opened the door. "How do you like it?"

Frank blinked as his eyes adjusted to the dim light in the shed. Then his jaw dropped.

"It's—it's—it's awesome!"

7 Tanks (A Lot)

Parked in the shed was something that looked like a cross between a tank and a boat, except that it also had wheels like a car. It was covered with a thin plate of light steel alloy, with one heavy deflector plate in the rear. A small cannon was mounted just behind the steel deflector, and a machine gun was on top of its center cockpit. A long metal battering ram stuck out up front like a big horn.

"I designed it myself!" The weapons supplier grinned. "I call it Rhino."

"Good name," Joe remarked, staring at the steel horn jutting from the strange contraption. "You mean, we're supposed to drive this thing into Zebwa?"

Charlie laughed. "I will show you how to operate it tomorrow morning. In it, you will be safe from any attack."

The portly man then pointed out some of the Rhino's other features. It was equipped with radar, with which they could track any large metal objects within a mile radius. It also had a smoke-screen device that could leave pursuers lost in a huge cloud of black smoke. On top of that, the Rhino was equipped with two roll bars, allowing it to turn over and over and still end up upright.

"And look here," Charlie said, stooping down underneath the back end of the vehicle and showing them a propeller blade. "The Rhino will run on water, too. You can make it work just like a speed-boat."

"You mean this thing floats?" Frank asked, doubt-fully looking at the steel-covered contraption.

"Oh, yes!" Charlie beamed with pride. "Very well!"

"Is that all it does?" Joe asked, half joking.

Charlie stroked his chin. "Let me see," he said, going down the list in his mind. "The cannon, the machine gun, the deflector, the smoke screen, the radar, the propeller—ah, yes! I forgot to tell you about the remote control."

The jolly African reached into the cockpit and

pulled out a pocket-sized electronic device. It resembled a simple television remote control, with several buttons and a miniature dial.

"With this, you can turn the Rhino on and off as well as maneuver it without having to be inside," he stated, handing the device to Frank. "Just like you do with a toy car or airplane."

"Interesting," Frank said, studying the small box. "But when would you ever want to use it?"

"Ha, ha, ha!" The man's jolly laugh bubbled up one more time, his belly bouncing. "I have no idea! I just threw it in for fun! I will show you how to use it and everything else in the morning. But now, get some sleep."

The Hardys followed the weapons supplier back to the house, where he showed them to his guest quarters and bid them good night. Both Chet and the Hardys were ready to sleep, but Niki couldn't, still troubled by her memories. To take her mind off them, Frank and Joe stayed awake and talked to her about their super van until she finally dozed off.

The next day Charlie taught all of them how to drive the Rhino and operate its various devices. By noon they had mastered it, including the cannon and the machine gun.

"Do you really think we'll have to use these things?" Frank asked, growing more uneasy by the minute.

"If you are lucky, you won't," Charlie replied.

"But you may. The Tota rebels have many tanks and guns. If they chase you, you will have to shoot back."

Frank wasn't the only one uneasy about the mission. Joe also became increasingly apprehensive, and Chet was a wreck. But Niki was determined to return to her people at Akutu's hidden encampment in the mountains, so the boys had little choice but to either go with her or let her go alone. And they weren't about to do that.

"Maybe it would be better if we entered Zebwa on foot," the dark-haired detective suggested. "It seems to me the Rhino would just call attention to us. If we were to hike through the jungle at night, maybe the rebels never—"

"No," Charlie answered firmly. "You will be much safer in the Rhino. Believe me."

After lunch, he outlined their route to Zebwa. They were to enter on the jungle side of the mountain range and follow it until they came to a deep river. There they would transform the amphibious vehicle into a boat and cross over, leaving any rebels who may have been after them unable to continue. Akutu's hidden camp would be only a few miles away.

"Now, you wait for dawn tomorrow," Charlie said, once the foursome had memorized his instructions. "You would lose your way in the jungle at night. Dawn is the best time, when the rebel border guards are asleep on their feet."

The second night at Charlie's house was a long one, and this time no one slept very much. While waiting for the first light to appear on the horizon, the young people had breakfast. Niki talked about her life—growing up in the palace with her father, his fight to improve Zebwa's standard of living, and how she had found Bobo in the desert when the chimp was just a baby. Bobo had been orphaned or abandoned by his parents, and she had taken him home to the palace and raised him.

"Tell us about Bidoli," Joe said. "You said you thought of him almost like an uncle?"

"I did." The pretty African girl sighed. "He was always very nice to me. But you'd be amazed what people will do for power in such an unstable country as Zebwa. Living in America, you might not believe that something like this could happen. But it can."

"Have you thought any more about that night?" Frank queried. "Do you still believe your father's killer came after you with a jewel-handled knife?"

Niki nodded. "I really remember it that way. It was right in front of my face when Bobo jumped the assassin. I don't understand it."

Neither did the Hardys, and they wondered if Bidoli had been given a fair trial. They listened as Niki described her life over the last two years. Having escaped her country, she'd headed north, finally making it to Europe. She'd lived like a tramp for months, penniless and on the run, working odd jobs, sleeping in train yards and alleys, until finally contacting her relatives in America, who sent her the money to fly over and join them. After a while, she had begun to feel safe again, so she decided to pursue a career as a fashion model, the first step of which was to win the beauty contest.

"But I always knew I'd have to return to Zebwa someday," she concluded. "It's in my blood."

Frank looked out the window. The night had been broken by a dim glow on the horizon. "Well, let's do it," he said, standing up.

Charlie had warmed up the Rhino's engine, and Joe took the wheel while Frank loaded the machine gun. Chet's job was to man the cannon, if necessary, and Niki would operate the radar.

"Good luck!" Charlie grinned as they started off heading east for the mountains. "And try not to wreck the Rhino!"

Once on their way in the bizarre amphibious vehicle, a thought occurred to the brothers. Perhaps their mission was serving a dual purpose the weapons merchant hadn't told them about. Maybe Charlie was just using them to deliver the Rhino to Akutu. That might explain why he'd insisted they not make the journey on foot.

"I say we ditch this thing," Frank said as they drew near the border. "I feel like a sitting duck."

"Too late now!" Joe blurted, putting the Rhino into high gear and stepping on the gas.

They had just rounded a bend in the road, and less than a hundred yards ahead was a rebel border patrol!

"Get down!" Frank shouted, ducking into the steel-plated cockpit at the same moment the patrol sergeant gave orders to fire.

Flying bullets pinged off the Rhino's steel plating as Joe plowed straight through the armed patrol, forcing the Tota rebels to dive off the road to avoid being hit.

"I hope that's the end of it!" Chet shuddered, once the barrage of gunfire had subsided behind them.

Frank peeked over the rim of the cockpit. The foot patrol was now out of firing range, but he could see the sergeant speaking into a walkie-talkie. "I think that was just the beginning," the dark-haired boy murmured.

"I'm getting bleeps on the radar!" Niki called out from her position below.

"Are they moving?" Joe asked, still racing down the dirt road at full speed.

Niki stared at the little electronic bleeps on the screen. "No, I don't think—wait! They're starting to move!"

"How far away?"

"Less than a mile!" the girl called back.

The morning sun had broken over the horizon and they saw that the foliage by the side of the road was growing denser. The mountains looming up on the left also seemed to be growing in size, their jagged peaks silhouetted against the sky.

"Man the cannon!" Frank ordered, grabbing the machine gun.

The cannon was about the size of a bazooka. Chet's hands shook when he took its controls so that he could hardly set the firing mechanism. When he finally had it ready and swiveled into position, it was almost time to use it.

"Here they come!" Joe yelled.

A cloud of dust was visible beyond a rise in the road ahead, indicating approaching vehicles. Frank pivoted his machine gun, leveling it at the top of the rise.

"How many are there?" he called.

"Three ahead! Two behind!" Niki replied. Frank glanced over his shoulder but saw nothing. Then he looked forward and noticed a spot where the jungle opened up on the left.

"What about to our left?" he asked.

"All clear!"

"Okay, let's see what this baby can do," Joe said, gritting his teeth.

The blond boy swung the wheel to the left just as two jeeps appeared at the top of the crest ahead. They were full of armed troops!

"At least they didn't come in tanks," Frank

muttered in relief, pulling the machine gun's trigger to return the fire that was already spewing from the rebels' guns.

But he had spoken too soon. The third vehicle appeared over the rise. And it was a tank. A moment later, two more came into view from the rear. Joe had gotten off the road just in time.

"I can't aim this thing!" Chet cried, trying to steady the cannon as the Rhino bounced roughly over the rocks hidden by tall grass.

Joe pulled a hydraulic lever that lowered a set of tank treads. In the same motion, the Rhino's wheels were drawn up. "Try!" he shouted back.

The rebel jeeps turned off the road in pursuit. Then came the tanks. Frank kept his machine gun leveled as best he could. He knew that because of the rough terrain, the jeeps would soon be dropping back. But the tanks were a different story. One well-placed shot from them could spell disaster.

BOOM!!

8 Rhino Power

Chet fired the cannon, wiping out a couple of palm trees at the edge of the open field.

"I told you I couldn't aim this thing. It's bouncing around all over the place!" he yelled.

"What do you want me to do? Stop?" Joe retorted frantically. "Just keep shooting! If you can't hit anything, you can at least scare 'em a little!"

Chet reloaded the miniature cannon as Joe zig-zagged across the open area to keep the rebel tanks from getting a good shot at them. The jeeps were already beginning to drop back, but the tanks were right on the Rhino's tail.

BOOM!!

Chet's cannon went off again, missing them by a mile. But the tanks returned the fire with better accuracy.

BOOM!! BOOOOOMMMM!!

Two shells exploded in succession, one tearing a hole in the ground the size of a small crater not twenty feet from the Rhino.

"Use the smoke screen!" Frank yelled, ducking shell fragments.

Joe flipped a switch on the control panel. A second later, thick black smoke spewed from the exhaust pipe.

"I can't see anything!" Chet cried as the Rhino was enveloped by a dense cloud.

"Good!" Joe responded. "That means they can't see us either!"

With smoke still gushing from the exhaust pipe, Joe maneuvered the Rhino in crazy patterns around the grassy field, totally obscuring the vehicle in the cloud as well as throwing the rebels into a state of confusion. Exploding tank shells still flashed all around like lightning in a fog, but none were as close as the first two.

"All right, you've dazzled them enough!" Frank commanded. "Now let's get out of here before we're surrounded!"

"How does it look on the radar?" Joe called down to Niki's station before picking a direction.

"They're closing in on all sides except the north!"
The African girl called back, "I see about twelve
more coming from the east and west!"

"Then we go north!" Joe stated, realizing their
only option was to head for the mountains. "Hold on
to your hats, kids!"

He switched off the smoke screen and gunned the
engines, aiming straight for a wall of jungle foliage
at the north end of the field. The Rhino's steel horn
penetrated the wall of brambles, and for a moment
everyone held their breath, fearing they would get
stuck. But the vehicle didn't stop. It plowed right
through the jungle wall and soon was bulldozing its
way over bushes, vines, and small trees.

Frank abandoned the machine gun and climbed
down into the cockpit to check the radar screen.

"We'd better pray we make it to the mountains
before the Totas catch up," he murmured to Niki, as
they both stared at the little dots of light marking
the encircling rebel forces.

The bleeps on the screen were closing in from
three sides, but the young detective was mostly
concerned about the tanks they'd left behind in the
field. While the troop-loaded jeeps were no longer a
threat, the tanks would be hot on their trail and
gaining fast since the Rhino had already cleared a
path into the jungle.

"I'm sorry about this mess I got you into," the
African girl apologized in a quivering voice. "I

should never have asked you to come. If I had known—"

"Hey, they haven't caught us yet," Frank said with a wink.

Frank gave Niki an assuring squeeze on the shoulder. But his mind was elsewhere. For the first time since the fighting began, he had a moment to think about it. While his own life had been in jeopardy many times already in his short career as a sleuth, until now he'd never actually fired a gun, much less a machine gun, on another human being. True, it was in self-defense and therefore justifiable, but it nonetheless was a jarring and troubling experience. Had he hit anyone? Had he killed anyone? He couldn't shake the empty feeling welling up in his gut as he gazed out at the jungle falling away behind him. Then he felt anger taking over. If they'd done it their own way instead of Charlie's, they would have gone unarmed, traversing the jungle on foot by night in the hope of not getting caught. But they'd done it Charlie's way, with bullets and cannon shells. It was the wrong way.

Frank shifted his gaze to Joe and Chet, who both seemed to be having similar thoughts as they stared blankly out upon the jungle. The sparkle of youth and innocence had already begun to drain from their eyes.

"Well, I hope they don't catch us," Niki sighed. "They're a nasty crew."

With Joe doing an expert job behind the wheel, the Rhino made it to the foot of the mountain range before the tanks could overtake it. Joe then traversed the bottom slope of one of the steep mountains until he found what he was looking for—a narrow canyon straight up into the range.

"Let's hope this takes us to the other side," he said. "It's our only chance."

The canyon wound up to higher elevations, leaving the jungle behind, and the Rhino made good time following its course. With fingers crossed, the group's hopes rose with the altitude. Soon they'd be over the hump and on the downslope into the desert side of the range.

"Are you picking anything up on the far side?" Joe called down to Niki.

"Nothing!" she responded gleefully, seeing not only that the desert side of the range was clear but also that the pursuing tanks were now so far behind they were dropping from the radar screen. "And the border is just a few miles away!"

Once over the range and near Zebwa's borders, the foursome would be safe and have time to rethink the whole operation. But looking ahead, they could see the canyon grow even narrower, with vertical cliffs rising up on both sides.

Suddenly, their hopes popped like a balloon as they rounded a new turn. The canyon came to a dead end at a fifty-foot wall of solid rock!

"I knew we'd get into trouble with this thing!" Frank growled in frustration.

Even if they were to set out on foot now, there was no way to go but back down the canyon.

"Why did you stop?" Niki cried from her station inside the cockpit. "I see the tanks again on the screen! They're coming closer!"

"Because we're trapped," Joe replied, his heart sinking.

The brothers realized why the rebels had been so slow in pursuit. They had purposely corraled them into the canyon, knowing it came to a dead end. There was nothing left for the foursome to do but surrender. They climbed out of the armored vehicle, raising their hands above their heads as the Tota tanks chugged up the canyon.

"Whatever you do, don't tell them who you are," Frank whispered to Niki, fearfully suspecting that the rebels would probably recognize her anyway.

Several armed troops emerged from the tanks, roughly taking the group hostage. Surprisingly, no one seemed to recognize Niki Jerusa, but the Hardys didn't expect their luck to hold out once they were taken to the rebels' headquarters.

"I demand to speak with the American ambassador!" Chet protested when he was being seized.

"Oh, we are so sorry," one of the Totas mocked the request in perfect English. "Your American ambassador is on vacation. A permanent vacation! Ha, ha, ha!"

89

After being frisked for concealed weapons, the group was forced back into the Rhino, and with rifles at their backs were directed to follow the tanks. An hour later, they found themselves at a military outpost in the mountains, where they were locked up in a makeshift jail cell and one by one taken to the commandant's office for questioning.

"Are you okay?" Niki asked, as armed guards ushered Joe back to the cell.

"I've been better," Joe responded with a weak grin as he leaned against the clay wall.

The blond boy's cheek was puffing up and an ugly bruise had formed below his right eye. He was the last to be questioned, and had been treated more roughly than the others. But the next round of interrogation, they knew, would be tough for everyone.

"Good," Frank sighed. "So far they just think we're working for Charlie as weapons suppliers."

Apparently, even the outpost commandant hadn't caught on to Niki's identity. That, plus the fact that the Rhino was parked just outside the commandant's office, had given Frank an idea.

"D-d-do you think they'll torture us?" Chet gulped, silently promising himself if he ever made it home alive, he'd never leave Bayport again.

"Not if my strategy works," Frank replied.

He quickly went over his idea before the guards came to start the second series of interrogation.

"Let me go first," he told the Totas. "I'm ready to talk."

With soldiers on either side, Frank was led across the hall again and into the commandant's office. The walls were made of the same mud clay as the walls in the cell, and Frank deduced that the structure had long ago been built by missionaries when the continent was first being explored. There was a window behind the commandant's desk, and Frank could see the Rhino parked outside not twenty yards away. The commandant himself was a trim, sinewy man in army fatigues, who studied his prisoner coolly from behind his desk.

"You say you are ready to talk. So talk."

Frank gazed over the man's shoulder out the window, mentally gauging the distance from the office to the Rhino. Then he looked into the commandant's eyes.

"I'll make you a deal. But only if you guarantee you'll set us all free—and unharmed."

"What kind of deal?"

"I'll tell you where Akutu's hideout is," Frank replied calmly. "And I'll also set things up so you can raid the camp with almost no resistance."

"How?" The commandant's tone was full of mistrust, and Frank knew he'd have to work hard to be convincing.

"There is a communication device in our tank," he said. "With it, I can contact Akutu and tell him we have been surrounded by the enemy and need assistance. That will draw the loyalist troops from the camp, leaving it wide open for a raid."

Frank knew full well that even if the commandant agreed to the deal, he would never set them free. He had planned accordingly.

The African commander ordered his guards to fetch the communication device from the Rhino, and a moment later they brought it in. It was, in fact, the armored vehicle's remote-control box!

"You can talk to Akutu with this?" the commander asked, taking the box and turning it over in his hand.

"No, but I can send a coded radio signal by pushing the buttons. It's a secret alphabet code Akutu uses to keep people like you from picking up his communications."

Again, the commandant's eyes fixed warily upon the young captive. Frank's stomach was by now a tight bundle of nerves and his body dripped with sweat under his cotton clothing. But he had to keep his cool or all would be lost. Having to improvise his plan as he spoke, he just kept talking and talking until the rebel commandant began to believe his story about being a greedy weapons merchant who wanted nothing but to save his own skin. Frank could have won an Academy Award for his acting job.

"Okay, you give me the code and tell me where the camp is," the African finally said. "We will mount a raid in a few days. Until it is successful, you will stay here."

"You have to strike now," Frank said flatly. "If Akutu doesn't hear from us today, he will suspect something and move his camp to another location."

The commandant was silent for a minute, considering whether he had enough troops to raid the loyalists' encampment right away. Then he ordered all his people at the outpost to prepare for an immediate assault.

"I will send the message now," he told Frank. "You show me what to do. If you try to deceive me, you will be shot."

Frank sighed and his stomach again went tight as he instructed the man which buttons to push. Between the noise of troops scurrying to prepare for battle, tanks being started up, and his concentration over the control box, the commandant never heard the Rhino start up and turn toward his office.

"Now push the right button," Frank instructed, "now the left." He glanced over the man's shoulder out the window, hoping the African would not look up.

"Okay, now turn the dial hard to the right and hold it there."

"This does not sound like a code signal!" the commandant snapped angrily. "I think you have been lying to—"

SMASH!!

The Rhino burst through the wall of the structure

at full tilt! With his instructions, Frank had made the commandant crank it up to top speed and aim it straight for the office! The clay walls crumbled on impact, and the commandant dove from its path as it flattened his desk and plowed right on through the next wall into the hallway. On its way, Frank jumped into the cockpit and switched it into manual override.

"Get in!" he yelled, after he crashed through the wall of the jail cell.

9 The Roar of Doom

Frank stopped just long enough for Joe, Niki, and Chet to climb aboard. Then, using the Rhino's steel horn as a battering ram, he smashed right through the far side of the cell and out into the open.

"Great move!" Chet exclaimed. "They never even knew what hit 'em!"

"Thanks, but we're not out of this mess yet."

Looking back, Frank could see the gaping hole the Rhino had punched into the clay building. Dazed guards poured out of the hole, coughing and choking in the dust and rubble. They were followed seconds later by the rebel commandant, who began shouting orders.

Frank slid over for his brother. "Take the wheel. You're better with this thing than I am."

Again at the controls, Joe gave it full power, steering the Rhino down the only road leading to the outpost. The road was very narrow and precariously cut into the side of a mountain. Below it, a shimmering river snaked through a deep gorge.

"Is that the river Charlie told us about?" the blond boy queried.

Niki nodded. "Yes. If we could follow it to the foot of the mountains, we'd be just a few miles from Akutu's camp."

Joe glanced to his right. The river flowed swiftly through the gorge, but it seemed deep enough to be navigable. And the slope, while steep, was both clear of obstacles and composed of the same soft mud clay with which the rebel outpost had been constructed.

"It's got to work," he muttered to himself, staring down over the precipice and gritting his teeth. "It's just got to work."

"Step on it! Here they come!" Frank shouted.

A caravan of tanks and jeeps was speeding along the road in pursuit and gaining rapidly. Seeing them, Chet frantically began loading the cannon.

"Forget the cannon!" Joe commanded.

"But they're catching up!" Chet argued, his voice cracking with fright. "What choice do we have? We can't just drive off this cliff!"

"Yes, we can! Get down in the cockpit and brace yourself!"

They all scrambled into the body of the Rhino, grabbing seat belts and shoulder harnesses. By the time they were strapped in, rebel gunfire was already pelting the vehicle's metal exterior.

"Hang on!" Joe warned, flipping a switch.

Two heavy steel hoops swung out and locked into place, encircling the Rhino's hull. Then Joe stepped hard on the brakes, throwing the vehicle into a skid right off the edge of the embankment. For ten seconds that seemed like forever, it tumbled like a big barrel down the slope to the river, its frame protected by the steel roll bars.

SPLOOOOSH!!!

The Rhino hit the river, spinning a few more times until it finally bobbed upright in the water.

"I don't believe it! It really floats!" Joe exclaimed, so dizzied by the wild tumble that he could barely see straight. "Is everyone okay?"

"For once I'm glad I missed lunch." Chet groaned. "'Cause it would've been all over the cockpit right now."

Joe grinned at his nausated friend, then peered out of the Rhino to the road above where the rebels had stopped. The rebels in their tanks were in the process of swiveling and aiming their guns toward the river.

"Let's get going. We're like ducks in a pond here," Frank uttered, fighting his own dizziness.

Joe quickly hit three more switches. The Rhino's treads were hydraulically pulled into its frame and the gear mechanism shifted to the propeller, transforming the vehicle into a power boat!

VROOOOOOOOOOM!!

The propeller churned in the water and spewed a jet of white foam from the Rhino's tail end.

"Haul it!" Chet shouted, seeing puffs of smoke issue from the rebel guns.

Plumes of water shot into the air as shells hit the river, but soon the Rhino had gained enough way to make it past the danger zone.

"That was way too close!" Frank sighed, looking back.

"Yeah," his brother agreed. "Now keep an eye out for rocks. This thing doesn't handle all that well."

Frank climbed from the cockpit and went forward to what was now the Rhino's bow. The river flowed swiftly, making the bizarre vehicle hard to control. But the main current seemed to follow a clear route between boulders, and Joe kept up just enough headway to give him adequate steerage through the rocks while Frank called out directions. After safely maneuvering around several bends, the boys figured the river would soon reach the base of the mountains and flatten out in the jungle. At that point, they'd be able to re-engage the Rhino's treads and drive the rest of the way to Akutu's camp.

"Do you hear that?" Niki asked, joining Frank at the bow as they were nearing what they hoped would be the last curve in the fast-flowing river.

The young detective cupped his ears and listened intently. A faint, low roar was coming from the other side of the turn.

"Pull over to the bank!" Frank bellowed, suddenly recognizing the sound. "There's a waterfall up ahead."

"I can't!" Joe yelled. "I don't have enough control. The current's too strong!"

The Rhino rounded the bend and the river seemed to drop off into nothingness less than a hundred yards in front of them!

"Does this thing have a parachute?" Chet gulped as his face turned a whiter shade of pale.

"No. Jump!" Frank cried. "Try to get to those rocks. Jump!"

Several large boulders jutted up from the river fifty yards before the lip of the falls. Without a second to spare, the foursome got out of the cockpit and dove into the water. They frantically swam through the swift current.

"Where's Chet?" Joe asked, alarmed, when he reached the rocks with Frank and Niki.

The Rhino had already been washed over the waterfall and disappeared into a roar of foam and spray.

"I'm here!" a youthful voice responded.

Chet appeared from the far side of the rocks, soaked to the bone and totally exhausted.

"For a second I thought we'd lost you!" The blond boy breathed with relief.

"So did I." Chet shuddered. He had grabbed the last boulder in the cluster.

Clinging to the rocks, the group was still some distance from shore, and they knew they wouldn't be able to hang on forever.

"What do we do now?" Niki asked, her voice trembling from the chilly water as much as from fright.

Joe scanned the riverbank. It was flat and also far enough down the mountain slopes for trees and jungle foliage to survive. He then gauged the distance from the rocks to shore. The current slacked off near the bank, but it was still strong enough to sweep an average swimmer over the falls before he could reach safety.

"Wait here," Joe replied, pushing off.

As captain of his high-school swim team and holder of the best time for the hundred-meter free-style, Joe was no average swimmer. He stroked through the water and made it to the riverbank. Once there, he rigged some sturdy vines into a life line. He tossed one end out to the rocks and pulled the others in, one by one.

By the time all were safely ashore, the sun was starting to set over the mountains. The temperature was dropping fast, and the group huddled together, shivering, wet and very tired.

Frank stood up and gazed over the falls. "Well, so much for the Rhino," he said with a shrug.

The armored vehicle, which had caused fortune as well as misfortune, was smashed to bits at the bottom of the waterfall.

Suddenly, the dark-haired sleuth's attention shifted to the far bank. "Duck!" he hissed, and crouched down behind a bush. Rebel jeeps and tanks were on the hillside overlooking the falls. They had been following the foursome's course along the river. Now they came to a halt and were surveying the wreckage at the foot of the waterfall.

"Do you think they spotted us?" Niki asked Frank as they huddled in the underbrush.

"No. They wouldn't be standing around if they had," he replied. "They think we went over with the Rhino."

Frank's hunch was right. A moment later, the rebels got into their jeeps and turned back up the road, evidently assuming their prisoners had been killed.

"At least we got rid of them!" Chet shivered. "But now what? I'm freezing."

"I know these falls," Niki stated. "Akutu's encampment shouldn't be more than four or five miles from here."

"Good. Let's go." Frank said.

With the girl in the lead, the group left the river and hiked into the jungle. Walking warmed them up a little, but as night descended, the temperature dropped even more. Their progress in the dark was slow as they worked their way through the dense foliage. The steady chirp of African crickets was only broken by the occasional roar of prowling jungle cats. Chet carried a pointed stick, constantly on the lookout for any signs of feline eyes shining in the night.

"There it is!" Niki exclaimed finally and pointed ahead.

After three hours, the foursome had reached the top of a ridge overlooking a hidden valley. A sprinkle of torch lights was visible under a large protrusion of rock.

"Welcome, Niki Jerusa!" a male voice hailed them from out of the dark. "I am glad you made it!"

The pretty African girl's face broke into a broad grin. "Hi!" she replied, concluding that the man was one of Akutu's patrol guards. "I'm glad I did, too."

The man stepped out of the jungle, and Niki's expression suddenly changed into one of terror!

"Bidoli!" she shrieked.

10 Jungle Encampment

The man who'd supposedly been shot for assassinating Niki's father stood before them like a ghostly apparition in the night. He was very thin, with skeletal features and deep-set eyes, but he was strong and lithe, too—like a cheetah. Two men flanked him with rifles slung over their shoulders.

Niki froze for an instant, then began backing away in terror as the men advanced on her.

"Niki, don't be afraid. I—"

Frank and Joe were both bursting with curiosity, but this was no time to ask questions. They leapt at the men, landing flying tackles on the two with the rifles and knocking them to the turf.

"Run!" Frank shouted to the African girl. "Now!"

Caught by surprise, Bidoli and his men were delayed long enough for Niki to take off down the hill. Chet, who—like the Rhino—was amazingly agile for his size, tore after her. The Hardys made sure their friends were out of sight before escaping into the jungle themselves. Then they dodged and weaved through the underbrush to avoid the gunshots that were sure to follow them. But none did.

"I thought he was supposed to be dead," Joe panted as they flew down the hill toward Akutu's camp.

"Maybe Niki made a mistake in identifying him," Frank speculated. "I hardly got a good look at the guy myself."

The combination of darkness and Niki's imagination might have been playing tricks on her. Perhaps the man they had just seen was a guard who bore a resemblance to her father's killer.

"Then again, it might well have been Bidoli," Joe muttered. "The story about his execution may have been pure invention."

"So what was he doing near Akutu's camp? And how did he know it was Niki?"

"Good question."

Absorbed in thought, Joe didn't notice a gigantic spiderweb stretched out between two trees and ran right into it.

"Yech!" He winced, struggling to disentangle himself.

The threads of the web were as tough as nylon, and as he pulled them off, the blond youth felt the sensation of little legs crawling up his back!

THWACK!

Just as the spider reached Joe's shoulder, Frank swiped it off and stomped on it.

"Thanks," Joe said and shuddered, staring at the remains of the biggest spider he'd ever seen. It had a leg span of over half a foot and a body the size of a mouse. Joe had no idea what kind it was, but he was sure it packed a mean bite.

"No thanks necessary." Frank chuckled. "I would've done the same for anyone."

The eighteen-year-old's face then flashed with concern. "I'm beginning to wonder if we're heading for another spiderweb that makes this one look like playtime," he said, referring to Akutu's camp.

"I'm having the same thought myself," Joe concurred. "Things aren't adding up like they're supposed to. Let's clear this with Niki before we all march into a trap."

The brothers continued down the hill in search of Niki and Chet, but by the time they arrived at the edge of the camp, they saw that it was too late for any reconsiderations. Niki and their friend had already reached the place and were surrounded by cheering troops.

"I suppose we didn't have anything to worry about after all," Joe said, seeing the men rejoice at the girl's presence.

Frank and Joe entered the camp and joined their companions, who were conversing with a big man in a military uniform. His most distinguishing feature was his shiny, bald head.

"You say you saw Bidoli outside my camp?" he exclaimed in surprise at the brothers' approach.

"Yes," Niki replied.

She introduced the man to the Hardys as General Akutu, and he shook their hands warmly, thanking them for their part in Niki's return. He then ordered a squad of his men to scour the hills for Bidoli.

"Shoot him on sight!" he commanded.

Once the patrol had disappeared into the jungle, Akutu spoke to Niki. "This is very bad!" He frowned dramatically. "The traitor is still alive. You are very lucky he did not shoot you."

Frank and Joe again recalled that Bidoli could have easily ambushed them if he'd wanted to. But he hadn't. More interestingly, the loyalist general didn't seem to doubt Niki's report—he seemed more surprised that Bidoli was close by than that he was alive.

"Where is the Rhino?" Akutu then changed the subject as they walked with him to his tent.

Niki explained about the waterfall, and this upset Akutu more than anything.

"I was counting on the armored vehicle to lead my forces into battle!" the hairless man fumed. "I am very disappointed."

106

"We think it was a very bad idea to put us in the Rhino in the first place," Frank remarked. "It almost cost us our lives."

"You were safer in the Rhino," Akutu snapped back, with more than a trace of hostility in his tone. "The jungle and mountains are full of bandits. If they had not gotten you, the lions and tigers would have. You were much better off in the tank. I am only unhappy that you were so foolish as to lose it."

"Bandits?" Joe queried.

"Yes. There are many of them. And they prey on us and the rebels alike, robbing and killing anyone just for the sport of it. You would never have made it here alive if you had attempted the trek on foot, especially since it seems now clear that Bidoli has become one of these bandits."

Joe's impulse was to challenge the man, but Frank gave him a glance which told him to bite his tongue. They would get nowhere by harassing Akutu in his own camp.

Once in the general's tent, the group sat down to supper. Frank and Joe listened quietly as Akutu spoke of his plans to overthrow the Totas and make Niki Jerusa his vice president. Except for the leader's anger over the news that his patrol had not found Bidoli, the meal went smoothly. When it was over, the boys were excused from the table. Akutu wanted to be alone with Niki to explain the details of his upcoming military campaign.

"I will see that you are escorted safely out of

Zebwa in the morning," he said as Frank, Joe, and Chet left his tent. "It is much easier to get out of the country than into it. Now sleep well."

A guard led the young detectives to another tent where empty cots had been set up. But the boys were still too uneasy and in no mood to sleep. They wandered through the camp, finding loyalist troops huddled around fires. Though none of them spoke English, Frank and Joe noticed some things which increased their concern. First of all, there were no civilians in the camp, only soldiers. Yet they had been told that Jerusa loyalists from all walks of life had sought refuge with Akutu! Secondly, while some of the troops were excited by Niki's return, others didn't seem to care at all. In fact, the morale of the camp seemed to be very low on the whole.

"This doesn't make sense," Joe said. "I thought they'd all be having the party of the century."

"I have the feeling a lot of these soldiers are mercenaries," Frank remarked.

Suddenly, cries of pain pierced the night!

"Where's that coming from?" Chet asked anxiously, noticing that the troops didn't even bat an eyelash at the horrible sound.

Frank broke into a trot toward a tent at the far end of the encampment. Upon reaching it, he parted its canvas flap and looked inside. A soldier was bound to a pole and stripped to the waist, while another man with a bullwhip flogged him mercilessly. Each crack of the whip brought a cry of pain along with a fresh, ugly welt on the man's back.

"That guy was on the patrol to search for Bidoli," Joe whispered.

"Yeah, and he's being flogged because they didn't find him." Frank grimaced.

The boys turned from the tent in disgust.

"Now it's clear to me why the morale around here is so low," Frank said. "Akutu is a cruel commander."

"We'd better go see if Niki is all right," Joe suggested.

"Right," Frank agreed.

"Hi!" Niki smiled, still at the supper table talking with the general. "I thought you would be in dreamland by now."

"Not yet." Frank smiled back, happy to see Niki was fine. Then he shot an accusing glance at Akutu. "We were watching one of your men being flogged. Did those orders come from you?"

The bald man bristled. "You are so naive. You have no idea what it takes to keep an army disciplined!" he snapped. "Now go to bed. This is not your battle. And this is not your country!"

The brothers backed out of the tent. Maybe Akutu was right. To command an army, harsh discipline was necessary at times. But from the low morale at the camp, it nonetheless seemed as if Akutu had carried it too far.

"He certainly didn't appreciate being questioned by us," Frank said when they were at last lying on their cots. "If we give him any more lip, he'll have us flogged, too!"

So far, Akutu had been tolerant of the boys for Niki's sake. But they knew they had been treading on thin ice and could not push it any further. At breakfast the next morning, they were quiet as the general ordered a jeep and guide for their safe departure.

"I'll miss you," Niki said and gave them each a hug and kiss before they got into the jeep. "When we are back in power and the country is at peace once again, you will have reason to be proud."

The beautiful African girl handed the boys a yellow kerchief to remember her by, then Akutu presented them with a handsome reward for their services—a pouch full of uncut diamonds! Joe thanked him, then got into the jeep with Frank, Chet, and their guide. Soon they were driving along a road through the mountains.

There were no signs of the Tota rebels anywhere, and they were soon over the range and in the desert again. The guide was to loop around and return them to their Landrover outside Zebwa's borders.

When they had gone over twenty miles into the desert, already the sun was beginning to bake the three boys. Then, for no apparent reason, the driver suddenly halted.

"Why are you stopping?" Chet asked nervously.

The man replied by drawing a revolver from under his seat and aiming it straight at Chet's heart!

11 The Desert Phantom

Though the man did not speak a word of English, his intentions were clear. He wanted the pouch of uncut diamonds that Akutu had given the boys as a reward. He snatched the bag from Joe, then, with a malicious wave of his pistol, signaled for the trio to get out of the jeep.

"All right, don't shoot," Frank said calmly as he picked up his canteen and stepped onto the hot desert sand along with his companions.

He was hoping the guide would let them keep the water, which might be their only chance of surviving in the desert. But the man forced him to drop it. With one well-aimed bullet from his gun, he pumped a hole right through it. He then drove away, leaving the youths standing in the desert as the last drops of water dribbled from the canteen and seeped into the sand.

"I wonder if this was his own idea or Akutu's," Joe growled, angrily watching the thief's jeep head back toward the mountains in a cloud of dust. Frank gazed at the broad expanse of parched desert.

"I just wonder how we're going to survive," he said helplessly.

Already weary from the adventures of the last few days, the youths scanned the desert. The sun was high in a cloudless sky, and the horizon rippled with heat waves rising out of the baked sand.

"We could head back to the mountains ourselves," Joe suggested, shading his eyes while peering at the distant range. "It'll take us all day and half the night, but it's still our best shot."

What Joe meant by "best shot" was that they stood less than a 50 percent chance of making it to the mountains alive. And even if they did, they'd only be returning to the heart of Zebwa and face capture by the rebels. It was, however, better than staying out in the desert, where death from thirst and exposure would be certain.

"You're right," Frank agreed, trying to be optimistic. "But let's angle off to the west a little so we can pick up the range closer to the border."

"I'm hungry," Chet complained forlornly. "And thirsty."

"Well, why didn't you say so?" Frank kidded his chunky pal to raise his spirits. "We passed a great hot-dog stand not too far from here where you can get a chili dog and a cold soda for under a buck."

Chet cracked a weak smile at the joke. But it was no laughing matter. The late-morning temperature was already up to a hundred degrees under the searing sun, and he was starting to feel tired in the oppressive heat. To make it on foot through the desert would take a minor miracle!

All three boys knew it was much better to travel by night when the desert cooled down, but by then they might well be too weak with hunger and thirst to get anywhere at all. Also, they would be able to see better in daylight, so they wouldn't end up walking around in circles. It was a tough call, but the balance tilted toward leaving right away, sun or no sun. If they could make twenty miles during the hottest part of the day, they'd be able to reach the mountains by nightfall.

Pacing themselves for the long haul, the boys started walking through the desert. By noon, the temperature had climbed to a hundred and fifteen, and the air was so dry that their lips were beginning to blister. It was all Chet could do to put one foot in front of the other and stay focused on Frank ahead of him. By two in the afternoon, the plump youth's face was breaking out in heat blisters and he could barely drag his feet over the sand.

Frank and Joe were also weakening, but still had

their wits about them enough to keep in the right direction. They occasionally glanced back at Chet, who wove unevenly along behind them, and their worries increased that he would drop from exhaustion. They wouldn't be able to carry him.

"Look, a shopping mall!" Chet cried suddenly, stopping and pointing at the horizon with a crazed expression on his face.

The Hardys exchanged concerned glances, afraid that their friend was starting to crack in the heat. Of course, there *was* no shopping mall. The heat waves rising from the desert and his strained mental condition had caused him to see a mirage. But through the rippling heat, Frank and Joe noticed that there was indeed a small cluster of huts less than a mile away.

"A shopping mall!" Chet repeated, breaking into a wobbling trot for the huts.

"It's only a tribal village," Frank informed his delirious chum. "But it still might save us!"

With burning feet, skin, and throats, the boys picked up their pace, hoping there would be food and water in the village. Yet, remembering the starving tribes they had passed on their way to Zebwa, they realized there was very little chance that any spare food or water would be available!

When they arrived at the mud huts, however, the trio's hopes quickly soared. The villagers were poor, but they were not starving. Instead of skeletal bodies and distended stomachs, the children who gathered curiously around the boys had thin but healthy physiques.

"Water!" Joe begged, miming the act of drinking so the youngsters would understand.

"Water?" a voice behind him asked. "You will have water."

Several adults had emerged from the huts, led by a toothless old man in a dirty robe and sandals. The boys were surprised that anyone spoke English.

"My name Heshee," the old man introduced himself with a toothless grin. "You come with me."

Frank wanted to ask the man why his people seemed to be so well fed. But his inquiries would have to wait. Right now his throat was burning. Water first. Questions later.

The threesome stumbled along behind him as he led them into one of the huts. Chet collapsed on a bed of reeds on the floor, where two women moistened his blistered lips and fed him small sips of water until he began to regain his senses. Frank and Joe also took clay pots full of cool liquid, pouring it down their parched throats.

"You saved our lives," Frank said to the old man. "How can we repay you?"

Their host grinned. "You just tell me why you here?" he said in broken English. "Why you in desert?"

Frank related the story of their mission and how they'd brought Niki into Zebwa.

"You bring Niki Jerusa back?" Heshee exclaimed delightedly. "That very good!"

In his own language, the old man related the news to the other villagers who had followed them into the hut, and soon the place was filled with excited chatter. When people finally calmed down, Heshee asked more questions.

"Where Niki now?" he wanted to know.

"We left her at the Jerusa loyalist camp, with Akutu," Joe repeated slowly, seeing that the man hadn't understood it the first time.

Heshee's expression suddenly dropped.

"With Akutu?" he exclaimed, anxiously waving his hands in the air. "That very bad! Very bad!"

The brothers had the feeling their welcome mat had just been rolled up. Again the old man translated for the villagers, who all began gesturing in alarm and again talked among themselves—only this time in troubled tones.

For the first time since their arrival, it dawned on the Hardys that they might not be among friends. For all they knew, the villagers could be working as spies for the Totas and were being supplied with food for their services. But there was another possibility, one so horrible that the boys could hardly allow themselves to think it. But it was the one most obvious explanation for the physical condition of the people in the village.

Cannibals?

"Akutu is bad?" Frank asked nervously.

"Yes! Yes! Is bad!"

Greatly agitated, their toothless host consulted with several other men, and after a minute turned back to his visitors.

"You stay. Rest here!" he commanded. "Do not go!"

The command was unnecessary. The boys were in no shape to go anywhere, especially Chet. For him to return to the desert now would be suicide. But Frank and Joe wondered what the villagers had in store for them. They looked for objects lying around the hut which they could use to defend themselves if necessary—hoping it wouldn't be a human thighbone!

"May I ask you one question?" Frank said as the old man started out of the tent.

Heshee gave the young American a wary look. "What do you want to know?"

"How come your people aren't starving? Does someone supply you with food?"

Frank could barely get the question out, but he had to know. Naturally, if Heshee and his people were indeed cannibals, they wouldn't tell their victims about it. But the way he answered the question was bound to reveal something.

"Yes! The Desert Phantom!"

With that, Heshee strode from the hut, leaving Frank now more curious than fearful. It didn't sound like a name for cannibalism. But what was it?

"Did he say the Desert Phantom?" Joe asked incredulously, when all the villagers were gone except two guards at the hut's entrance. "Who in the world is the Desert Phantom?"

"I think we'll have the chance to find out." His brother sighed. "Now let's get some rest like the old man said. I have a feeling this is going to be a long day."

"Follow me!" a voice woke them after a good two-hour nap. It was Heshee, standing at the door of the hut in his robe and sandals.

Frank and Joe stood up and helped Chet to his feet. Their friend was almost back to normal. Since it was now late in the afternoon, the temperature had cooled considerably, which made them all feel better.

"I'll be okay." Chet grinned. "Hey, aren't you guys glad I spotted this great shopping mall?"

"Come," Heshee ordered, walking out of the village.

With no idea what awaited them, the youths followed the old man due west into the desert, toward the setting sun.

"Maybe we should ditch him," Joe whispered, sidling up to Frank once they were alone with Heshee. "Chet's strong enough now to make it the rest of the way to the mountains, and it should be a lot easier by night."

"I say we go along with this," Frank whispered

119

back. "I think he's taking us to the Desert Phantom, whatever—or whoever—it is."

"Stop here!" Heshee ordered when they'd hiked about three miles.

The group had reached a tiny hillock covered with withered bushes. The sun was now below the horizon and the sky had turned a deep shade of purple.

"Why are we—"

Joe didn't have time to finish his sentence before seven masked men jumped up from behind the bushes. They were dressed in rags, unshaven, and had rifles slung over their shoulders. In seconds, the boys were surrounded.

"Bandits!" Joe gasped.

12 The Cave

The ambush had been a setup. That much was obvious. But why had Heshee led them into it? The Hardys didn't dare move as they were surrounded by the ragged men and blindfolded along with Chet. With rifles at their backs, they were then prodded toward an unknown destination.

Unable to see, Joe could still feel the chill of night descend around him as they marched single file over the sand. "Are you taking us to the Desert Phantom?" he asked.

He got his answer—a sharp jab from a rifle barrel in his lower back. The bandits wanted no questions, only obedience. In silence, Joe continued walking and was beginning to weary when he suddenly felt the air temperature drop another ten degrees and heard his footsteps start to echo. They had entered a cave.

"Loo abba zin wastago! Deeba wan Hardy boys!" a Zebwanese voice commanded.

Frank, Joe, and Chet were brought to a halt at a point where a dim flickering light filtered through their blindfolds, which were suddenly removed.

"Bidoli!" Frank uttered, blinking from the glare of torchlight.

The bony man whom the Hardys had encountered in the jungle the night before sat on a makeshift stone throne in the center of a large cavern. Burning torches lined the cavern walls and twenty or more armed men clustered about the boys, grim and unspeaking.

"Are you the Desert Phantom?" Joe asked, uneasily meeting Bidoli's gaze.

There was no trace of friendliness in the assassin's eyes as he nodded in reply. "Yes," he said, this time in English. "I am the one they call the Desert Phantom. Now I ask the questions. Sit."

At Bidoli's command, the three boys were virtually shoved to the dirt floor of the cave by the armed outlaws. And as they sat, Frank noticed another man standing behind Bidoli.

It was the baby-faced man from Paris!

"You're the guy who tailed us!" Joe cried, also

recognizing the man who'd ripped Michelle's sequined glove off.

"I told you that I ask the questions!" Bidoli snapped.

One of the armed bandits swiped the back of Joe's head with the butt of his rifle, and the boy's first impulse was to jump the man. But he took the blow without even a wimper, controlling both his temper and his tongue.

"You have caused me too much trouble already," Bidoli growled. "Now talk! Tell me why are you here? And do not lie!"

The Hardys sensed that they were on trial and that any twists in the truth might cost them their lives. Choosing his words carefully, Frank explained how Mantu had hired them to locate Niki Jerusa, then to bring her to Akutu's camp. Though he brimmed with questions of his own, he didn't dare press Bidoli. He didn't have to. After detailing their mission, the supposedly dead assassin was beginning to relax, especially after hearing the boys' suspicions concerning Akutu.

"Akutu has made fools of you," Bidoli said, the hostility now gone from his tone. "I am sorry I had to treat you so roughly, but I had every reason to believe you knew what you were doing. I am not a traitor and I never assassinated anyone," he spoke firmly. "I ran from Jerusa's palace with everyone else the night of the revolt. I did not even know about the assassination until later when I discovered I was being hunted as the killer."

"Why does everyone think you were executed?" Joe queried, withholding judgment on the man's claim of innocence.

Bidoli grinned faintly. "I rigged that myself so they would stop hunting me. It was very easy to do. I found a dead man in the jungle who had been shot by the rebels and I dressed him in my uniform. By the time the body was found, it was so badly decomposed it could only be identified by the uniform. Everyone thought it was me and that I was dead. I then went into hiding and have since gathered a band of men who believe in my innocence. We have had to live like outlaws to avoid being captured and shot by the Totas."

"So you think you were framed?" Frank asked.

"I know it," Bidoli replied simply. "And I am sure that Akutu was behind it. He was the one who accused me and also the one who said he found my knife in Jerusa's bedroom. The fact is, I lost my knife when I fled from the palace the night of the revolt. One of the Tota rebels was chasing me and I had to defend myself. I threw the knife at him and ran. Anyone could have picked it up and put it in Jerusa's chambers."

Whether they'd been duped by Mantu and Akutu or not, the Hardys were not about to be taken in again by Bidoli. But his story seemed to jive with Niki's. She had remembered the murder weapon as

124

being jeweled, unlike Bidoli's, so it was very possible that the knives were switched after the killing to make Bidoli look guilty.

"Is there any way to prove your innocence?" Joe posed.

Bidoli shook his head slowly. "How could I? I couldn't go back to the palace to look for new evidence. The rebels had ransacked it. My only hope was to find Niki. If I could make her believe I didn't kill her father, then maybe she would convince the people. It was my only hope. That's why I was so angry at you two for getting in my way."

The discussion turned to the baby-faced man who'd followed the boys to Paris. His name was Lyon, and he wasn't a rebel spy at all, but had been sent by Bidoli to follow Mantu and hopefully get to Niki first. When Lyon found out that Mantu had hired the Hardys to take up the search, he'd broken into their home, planted tiny electronic homing devices in the heels of their shoes, and listened in on their phone conversation with Mr. Hardy to make certain they were taking the case.

"So that's how you did it," Joe said and shrugged at the man behind Bidoli. "But how did you know which shoes we were going to wear?"

Lyon smiled proudly. "I put bugs in all your shoes. That way I was able to follow you no matter which pair you wore. The devices were only activated when you were walking, therefore only the shoes you had on gave off a signal."

"And that is how we found you in Paris as well as in the jungle last night," Bidoli told them.

Frank and Joe had to compliment Lyon on his ingenuity, but they also wondered why he hadn't just come forward and told them why it was important for him to find Niki before Mantu did.

"If he had, would you have gone on with the search?" Bidoli asked. "I think not, because you then would not have known whom to believe, Mantu or Lyon."

"You're right." Frank sighed. "We would've called it off."

Bidoli nodded. "You see, Mantu hired you because he wanted to throw Lyon off his trail. He knew that Paris was a dead end and that it would occupy both Lyon and you while he was searching for Niki in the Bayport area, where he had heard she was living."

"Where is Mantu now?" Frank asked.

"Probably in Akutu's camp," Lyon replied.

"What do you think Mantu would have done if he had found Niki first?" Chet asked.

"Killed her if she knew who her father's real assassin was," Bidoli answered matter-of-factly. "The story he told you about needing her to help rally the people's support was only half true."

"Do you believe that *Mantu* was the murderer?" Joe inquired.

"I do. But since Niki does not know that, I think

she is safe. For the time being she is more useful to him alive than dead."

"We still have to get her out of there!" Chet exclaimed.

"That is what I hoped you would say," Bidoli replied. "With your help, we may have a chance."

"But what was Akutu's motive?" Joe pressed.

Bidoli scratched his head. "I am not sure. Maybe he made a deal with the Totas and they reneged on it. Akutu had always been power hungry and ruthless."

"I bet the guide who stole our reward acted on his orders," Chet said. "He probably had no intention of letting us have the diamonds. He just wanted to put on a good show to help convince Niki."

"And he knew that I was still alive," Bidoli added. "No doubt he planned to pin your deaths on me."

"And Niki would have believed it along with everyone else," Joe said.

"Akutu put you in the armored vehicle to make sure I would not get my hands on you," Bidoli went on. "Much better the rebels either captured or blew you all up with tank shells than having me find you in the jungle. At least then, Niki would become a martyr for Akutu's cause instead of an instrument in his downfall, as she would have if I convinced her that Akutu was really the traitor."

"We've been fooled!" Joe said in disgust. "Now we have to make up for it and get Niki out of Akutu's camp!"

"I agree," Bidoli said. "But Akutu's forces out-number my men a hundred to one. Our only chance is for you to go back and convince Niki that I am innocent. Maybe she can then turn the real Jerusa loyalists against him."

Frank winced. "That's risky. Akutu probably wouldn't let us alone with her for a minute. And I doubt we could convince her without any proof."

Bidoli stood up, throwing his hands in the air. "Proof? How? What kind of evidence could we find? Even Niki, who is the only witness, cannot identify the real assassin!"

Just then, Heshee, who'd been patiently listen-ing, stepped forward. "Niki not the only witness," he said with a twinkle in his eye. "There also Bobo, the pet chimp."

Bidoli looked at the old villager as if he had lost his mind. "Do not be absurd! A monkey cannot be a witness."

"Why not?" the old man persisted. "Chimpan-zees have keen noses and good memories. He remember assassin by smell."

Frank and Joe gazed dumbfoundedly at the tooth-less villager. Maybe Bobo couldn't be considered a witness in a court of law, but if he reacted violently to Akutu's scent, it might be enough to convince Niki!

"But how could we possibly find Bobo?" Joe asked. "He's been missing for two years! He could be anywhere right now!"

Heshee broke out in a wide grin. "Leave to me. I need jeep, apple, and big rock of salt."

All were silent for a moment. Then Bidoli spoke up.

"If it were anyone but you, Heshee, I would think you were crazy," he said respectfully. "But you have surprised me before with your wisdom. You will have your jeep, and your apple, and your salt."

13 The Giant Anthill

Bidoli and his men had few resources, but they did have an old army jeep which they'd captured from the Tota rebels. They also managed to hunt up the hunk of salt and a small apple.

"You go in the morning with Heshee," Bidoli instructed the young detectives. "Now sleep!"

Bedding down on soft animal furs, the boys woke up to the pink light of dawn glowing through the mouth of the cavern. After a quick breakfast, they uncovered the jeep, which was concealed beneath a mound of brush near the hideout, and took off eastward across the desert with Frank at the wheel and Heshee beside him giving directions.

"Secret springs are in desert that only chimpanzees know about," the villager explained. "In summer and season of drought, many of them gather at springs for water and shelter, and they very careful not to let humans know where springs are."

"So you think Bobo might be at one of these hidden springs?" Joe asked.

Heshee nodded. "Yes. Bobo too tame to live in dangerous jungle on other side of mountains. He would go to spring where he would be safe among his own kind."

"But how do you know which spring it might be?" Chet questioned. "And if they're so secret, how are we supposed to find it?"

"Bobo would go to spring close to where palace is," Heshee stated. "That is why I brought apple and salt. You will see."

"Close to the palace?" Frank queried. "Won't that whole area be swarming with rebels?"

Heshee nodded. "But we still be far out in desert, miles from palace. Not likely we will be seen. But we must be careful and keep eyes open."

Joe pressed Heshee about what he was planning to use the apple and salt for, but seeming to delight in keeping the youths mystified, the villager told him only that it was an old trick he had learned. "You will see," he repeated with a grin.

Heshee had Frank stop the jeep at a desert lake

bed, where he checked the soil for moisture. "There is spring not far from here," he announced, returning with a clump of soggy sand in his hand. "This is good place to start. Palace just on the other side of mountains."

The Hardys looked toward the mountains, but saw no sign of the palace nor the capital city in which it was supposedly located.

"No worry. It there." The old man smiled. "Hidden by mountains."

Before dropping his clump of sand, Heshee ran his fingers through it one more time. His eyes suddenly twinkled as he then drew at what looked like a tiny round pebble from it. "Look!" he said, holding it up between his thumb and forefinger. "Fish egg!"

Frank and Joe glanced at each other, beginning to doubt the old man's sanity again.

Heshee laughed and placed the tiny egg in Joe's palm. "We sometimes find eggs in dry lake beds. They sit in sand like this for months, or years, then when rains come and lake fills up, eggs hatch and little fish swim out!"

"That's incredible!" Chet beamed, taking the egg from Joe and examining it. "You mean this egg can still hatch?"

"Yes," the man replied. "Here, you put in pocket and take home to America with you. Drop in bowl of water, and in no time you will have a fish!"

"Instant aquariums!" the chubby boy exclaimed, his eyes suddenly lighting up as if he'd struck gold. "I bet I can make a million bucks with this!"

Frank chuckled. "Let's forget the fish egg for now. We have to find Bobo."

The villager got back into the jeep and told Frank to continue toward the mountains. As they rode, Chet excitedly asked Heshee to send him all the dry fish eggs he could find and promised the old man 50 percent of his profits in return.

"We'll both be rich!" Chet exclaimed. "You find the eggs and I'll take care of sales! Our instant aquariums will be the hit of the year!"

Chet was always interested in get-rich-quick schemes, and for a while he was so thrilled by his idea that he completely forgot the reason why they were out in the desert. It was not until Frank braked near a huge anthill that the boy's attention was drawn from his fish egg.

"What are we stopping here for?" he asked.

"I will show you," Heshee answered. He stepped from the jeep and walked up to the giant anthill.

Made of hard mud baked under the desert sun, it stood almost eight feet in height and was wider than an old oak tree at its base. The colony of large black ants that had once lived in it were long gone, leaving only the mound of dried mud with a maze of tunnels bored into it.

Frank, Joe, and Chet watched with wonder as Heshee began dancing in a circle around the anthill and chanting in a strange, high-pitched voice.

"What is he doing?" Joe asked, scratching his head. "That's got to be the weirdest thing I've ever seen."

"That goes for them, too," his brother said, pointing to the branches of several leafless trees near the hill.

Monkeys of all different sorts had collected there, including chimpanzees. Naturally curious, the animals had been following the jeep through the desert and were now chattering excitedly at the sight of Heshee prancing around like a madman. Apparently, the villager's act was designed to attract their attention.

"He's not so crazy after all." Joe grinned as the old man stopped his wild antics.

With a captive audience of monkeys watching from the trees, Heshee took the apple from his hip pouch and placed it in one of the holes bored in the anthill. After that, he climbed back into the jeep.

"Drive away!" he said.

Now totally mystified, Frank started up the jeep and moved from the vicinity of the anthill.

"What was that all about?" Chet asked when they had driven a good half mile.

Heshee raised his finger into the air. "First we catch chimp. Then we make him thirsty so he runs to secret spring so fast that he not care if we follow."

The Hardys were beginning to understand the villager's plan. After ten minutes, they drove back to the anthill, and sure enough, one of the chimps was trying to remove the apple. But he couldn't—the hole Heshee had picked was just big enough to hold the apple. The chimp had clamped his fist over it, and now could not pull it out of the hole. It looked as if a small child had grabbed a bunch of cookies from the jar only to find he had taken too many to get his hand out.

"Watch," Heshee said with a wink and strolled toward the chimp. "This is what makes people smarter than monkeys."

The animal saw Heshee coming and turned to run, but was not ready to let go of the apple and free its hand. So, with its arm still stuck in the anthill, the old man was able to walk up close enough to slip a rope leash around the chimp's neck. Only then did the monkey forget about the apple long enough to let go of it and free its hand. But it was too late!

With the chimp on one end of the leash, Heshee tied the other end to a tree branch. Then he pulled the lump of salt out of his pouch and set it down in front of the monkey. Again he walked away.

"They love salt," he explained once he was back

in the jeep. "We leave now for a few hours. When we come back, salt will be gone."

The group drove off again and found a shady spot to enjoy a picnic lunch. When they were finished eating, they drove back to the anthill. The chimp had devoured the entire hunk of salt and was almost delirious with thirst.

"Now we let him go," Heshee said. "He will lead us straight to nearest spring."

The villager untied the chimp's leash and the thirsty animal started off at a full clip, making a beeline for one of the secret water holes without looking back.

Before long, the boys saw it disappear between a cleft in a small outcropping of rocks.

"There is spring!" Heshee announced, his voice ringing with pride.

"Thanks," Frank uttered. "Now let's hope your hunch about Bobo was right."

Stooping to get through the cleft, the boys followed Heshee into a small hidden clearing. Too busy quenching its thirst to notice them, the chimp they'd tailed had its face buried in a deep puddle of fresh water, which bubbled up from a crack in the rocks. But the other thirty or more chimpanzees gathered in the clearing began chattering and frantically waving their arms in alarm!

"No worry. They will not attack," Heshee said. "They just try to scare us."

Scanning the collection of chimps, Frank and Joe

136

looked for one which might be Bobo. They narrowed their search to several older animals perched on a ledge, knowing that Niki's pet had to be quite old by now.

"Bobo!" Joe called out, hoping that one of the monkeys would recognize the name. "Bobo! Bobo!"

But none of the chimps responded. In fact, none of them seemed the least bit tame or comfortable with humans. They all just went on chattering and waving at the strange beings who had invaded their water hole.

"Look!" Chet cried suddenly and pointed to one of the animals. "That one's wearing a ring!"

The brothers focused on a big chimp with a thin gold ring on his little finger.

"Remember what Niki told us?" Joe cried out excitedly. "She had been wearing a gold ring when Bobo bit off her finger. Maybe he kept it as a memento!"

"That's a real possibility!" Frank agreed.

The two boys slowly approached the chimp on the ledge, repeating the name Bobo over and over.

But instead of warming up to them, the animal fearfully climbed up the rocks and tried to get away.

"I have an idea," Frank said. "Joe, go to the jeep and get that kerchief Niki gave us when we left Akutu's camp. It's in my bag. Maybe the monkey will recognize her scent."

"Here it is!" Joe said a few minutes later when he returned with the yellow piece of cloth.

Frank wadded it into a small ball and threw it on the ledge. The chimp did not dare touch it at first, but, overcome by curiosity, finally picked it up and held it to its nose. It sniffed again and again, until a light flickered in its eyes.

"He Bobo!" Heshee called out, his own eyes shining happily. "He Bobo!"

14 Battle Zone!

As if by magic, Bobo slowly transformed from a wild animal into the tame pet he had once been. The chimp seemed to sense that the boys were there to take him back to Niki, and soon he was eagerly walking with them to the jeep, holding on tightly to Chet's hand as they went.

"Bobo like you!" Heshee laughed as the two climbed into the back seat together. "You his friend."

"Animals have an instinct for knowing who they can trust," Chet stated smugly. "So Bobo naturally came to me."

Swinging the jeep westward, Frank grinned back at his friend. "More likely you remind Bobo of his natural mother," he joshed.

"You're just jealous," Chet retorted. "Now let's get out of here before the rebels spot us."

An hour later, the Hardys, Chet, Heshee, and Bobo drove up to Bidoli's cave. Delighted that they'd found the chimp, the Desert Phantom immediately set about devising a plan.

"You boys must return to Akutu's camp with Bobo. Pretend you walked all the way from the desert. Accuse Akutu of nothing. Leave that to Bobo. And make sure Niki and the soldiers are watching when Akutu and Bobo meet. Understand?"

The boys nodded.

"I will be nearby with my men," Bidoli went on. "We will do what we can to help. But remember, Akutu has far more soldiers than I."

Deciding it was best to act quickly, Bidoli ordered his men to clean their rifles and fill their ammo belts while he went over the details with Frank and Joe. When all was ready, they bid good-bye to Heshee and set off toward the mountains—the boys in the jeep with Bidoli and his troops following on foot.

Night was again falling and the temperature had dropped by the time the jeep arrived at the base of the mountain range and went up the winding dirt road that the guide had used to transport the boys from Akutu's camp.

"You must walk the rest of the way," Bidoli said at the top of the first ridge. "Akutu has scouts beyond this point who watch the road day and night. Cut across to the next ridge and follow the canyon south. You will run into the camp in about three or four miles. And take your time. My men must have a chance to catch up."

"How will we know when your men are in position?" Frank asked.

"You do not. Signals would be too dangerous. But we will be ready when you get there. Just do not walk too fast."

Gripping Chet's hand, Bobo began to chatter nervously as he was led into the darkness. Whether he was frightened or excited the boys couldn't tell, but they did know that if the chimp suddenly refused to go on, there wasn't much they could do about it. Luckily, though, Bobo made no attempt to flee as they hiked over to the jungle side of the range and up the canyon.

"Well, here goes." Joe sighed when they finally reached the edge of the loyalist camp. "Let's ham it up good."

Akutu's troops had just eaten supper and were relaxing around campfires when Frank and Joe stumbled out of the jungle, carrying on like they were dying of thirst. Chet stayed hidden among the foliage with Bobo, waiting for the Hardys' rantings to have the desired effect. They did. Frank and Joe flopped dramatically to the ground and were soon surrounded by fifty or more soldiers.

"What is going on?" a booming voice demanded. The troops parted and Akutu strutted into the crowd. "It is you!" he exclaimed in surprise, staring down at the two sleuths writhing in the dirt in mock agony. "Where did you come from?"

"Your guide stole our reward and left us in the desert to die," Joe choked. "Water. Please give us water."

"He did what?" the baldheaded general shouted, faking anger. "I will have him shot for this!"

Playing innocent, Akutu ordered his men to execute his order. Then he had Frank and Joe taken to his tent.

"Where's Niki?" Frank rasped, still pretending to be on the brink of death as he was lifted by several soldiers.

"Taking a nap," the bald man spoke abruptly. "You will see her later."

Chet peered anxiously through the bushes as the men began to carry the Hardys away. "Come on, Niki," he muttered under his breath. "Where are you?"

According to the plan, Niki was supposed to be with Akutu when he found Frank and Joe. Only then was Chet to step out of the jungle with Bobo. Niki would recognize her pet chimp, and when

142

Bobo reacted to the sight of Akutu, it would prove to her and all the loyalist troops that the general was really the traitor. But Niki was nowhere in sight!

Chet groaned. There was no sign of Bidoli and his men, either. "What are we going to do?" he stammered as if Bobo could provide an answer.

The chimpanzee sensed that things were not going right and began chattering nervously as they both watched Frank and Joe disappear into Akutu's tent.

"I know." Chet frowned. "I'm worried, too."

Inside the tent, the Hardys were developing an alternate plan in their heads. They signaled each other with their eyes. As they had expected, Akutu wanted to question them in private, and once the troops had placed the boys on cots, he ordered his men to leave.

"Where is your fat friend?" the general asked the Hardys after they had satisfied their thirst from his canteen.

Still feigning delirium, Frank forced a tear to run down his cheek. "Out in the desert," he replied weakly. "He didn't make it."

"Oh, I am so sorry," Akutu replied, barely able to conceal a grin beneath his phony sympathy. "It is lucky that you are in better shape."

Joe lay stretched out on the cot as if unable to move. From the corner of his eye, he could see the general standing over him. "More water," he begged. "Please. More water."

143

Akutu leaned closer, his knees now just a few inches from Joe's face, and tipped his canteen to the sleuth's lips. But Joe never took the water. Instead, his arm uncoiled like a cobra and he snatched Akutu's wrist, twisting it with all his might!

Before Akutu could cry out, Frank leapt off his own cot and leveled the man, pinning him to the floor while Joe covered his mouth. A look of both surprise and intense hatred filled the general's eyes as he struggled to free himself.

"What have you done with Niki?" Frank asked evenly, knowing the story about her nap was a lie. "And don't try any funny stuff, because you'd be history by the time your guards got here. You understand?"

Fear began to register on Akutu's face as Joe shifted to an illegal wrestling hold—a choke-hold that could snap the man's neck in an instant with the right pressure!

"I—I told you she is resting," the general gasped, once allowed to talk. "I do not know what you have been told, but I promise I will not have you punished if you let me go right now. Just let me go and all will be forgotten."

Joe tightened his hold, all but cutting off the general's air passage. "Tell me what you did with her!" he snapped.

Just then, Frank heard a dull thumping noise come from a corner of the tent, where canvas tarps

144

and assorted supplies were stacked up in a huge pile. "You got him?" he asked his brother.

Joe nodded, also staring at the mound of military supplies. "I got him."

Letting go of Akutu, Frank started throwing things off the pile. At the bottom, he found a large footlocker and lifted its lid.

"Niki!" he cried.

The pretty African girl was crammed into the footlocker, her hands and feet bound with rope and a wad of cloth stuffed into her mouth! Luckily, there were air holes in the footlocker, so she was still alive. Frank quickly pulled her out and untied her. She was in shock and almost too weak to stand.

Joe tightened his choke-hold on Akutu. "Resting, huh?" he spoke through clenched teeth. "I'd like to give you a permanent rest, mister!"

Using Niki's ropes, the Hardys quickly tied and gagged Akutu. By the time they were finished, Niki was able to talk. "Thanks," she gasped, still shaky. "I thought it would be the end of me."

Joe helped her over to one of the cots. "What happened?" he asked.

"After you left, I became suspicious of Akutu," Niki explained. "I began to search through his belongings and found the jeweled knife that had been used to kill my father. I recognized it immediately."

"So you accused Akutu and he stuffed you in the footlocker," Frank said.

"Yes. He wanted me alive until he could find some way to dispose of me without his troops knowing," Niki confirmed. Then she looked curiously at the brothers. "What made you return?"

The boys knew they risked discovery at any moment, but they also wanted to be certain Niki was fully recovered before making their escape. So they quickly recounted the events of the past two days—from Heshee, to the Desert Phantom, to Bobo.

"You really found Bobo?" Niki beamed.

"He's outside the camp with Chet right now," Frank assured her. "Bidoli should be there, too."

He looked at the baldheaded general who, gagged and bound, could do no more than glare maliciously at the youths.

"Should we leave him here?" Niki shivered.

Joe shook his head. "We'll take him hostage. The only way to get out of here in one piece is to convince his troops that he's the real traitor."

"But are you sure they'll believe us?" the African girl asked uneasily. "And even if they did, would they turn against Akutu? Over half of them are mercenaries, you know."

Frank winced. "I know. We'll have to take that chance."

The bald man's eyes lit up. Apparently, he was convinced their plan would backfire. And the sleuths knew he might well be right!

"Okay, let's go," Joe ordered, untying Akutu's feet and ungagging him. "March!"

With Niki in the lead, the Hardys shoved the general from the tent and walked him straight out into the middle of the encampment. At first, the soldiers didn't seem to know how to react. It was toward the end of their evening meal and many of them were still busily polishing off plates of fried bananas and canned hash. Others, having finished eating, were now relaxing around campfires, sipping coffee. All were taken by complete surprise. In disbelief, they gawked at their captive leader for a moment, then a wave of alarm slowly began to erupt throughout the whole camp. Dropping their mess kits, the soldiers jumped to their feet and grabbed their rifles. Seconds later, Frank and Joe found themselves surrounded by a forest of bristling gun barrels—aimed, cocked, and ready!

"Don't shoot!" Niki commanded. "Don't shoot! Let me explain!"

"Shoot them now!" Akutu snarled, struggling in Joe's clutches. "They are traitors!"

For one tense moment, the boys held their breath, expecting to be riddled with bullets like Butch Cassidy and the Sundance Kid. But that moment passed quickly. The soldiers didn't fire.

They didn't lower their guns, either.

Niki knew she'd have to talk fast. She held the dagger high over her head for all to see, its jeweled handle refracting the light from the campfires. "This is the weapon that killed my father!" she boomed in a voice loud enough for all the soldiers to hear. "I know because I was there!"

"She's lying!" the baldheaded general bellowed.

"I'm not lying!" Niki answered back as Joe silenced the general by slapping a hand over his mouth. "I caught the assassin red-handed in my father's bedroom! I couldn't see his face because he wore a mask, but I remember this knife as if I had seen it yesterday. It was the same knife the assassin then tried to use to kill me! It is Akutu's knife!"

Angry murmurs broke out among the troops as Niki went on with her story, and the Hardys could see that the soldiers were already starting to divide. Some seemed to believe Niki, others were skeptical, and still others clearly preferred to shoot first and ask questions later. Tension mounted with every second as Niki went on with her story about the fateful night and how Bobo had ended up saving her life.

"Bidoli was not the assassin!" the African girl concluded, waving the dagger over her head. "It was Akutu himself! And this was the knife he used! The same one I just found in his tent! Akutu has been lying to you all along! All he wants is power! He cares nothing for Zebwa or its people!"

These last words had just the effect the boys had hoped for. The whole camp was on the brink of pandemonium. Heated arguments broke out among

148

the ranks, soldier against soldier, as to whether to believe Niki or not. All it would take was one final spark for the troops to turn their guns on each other.

"*EEEEaaaaeeeee!*"

An inhuman shriek split the night suddenly and all eyes shifted to a chubby boy and a chimpanzee who just walked out of the jungle—Chet and Bobo. Shrieking again, the chimpanzee flew at the general with a viciousness that surprised even the Hardys, and it was all the boys could do to prevent the enraged animal from injuring the man.

"Bobo!" Niki cried. "Bobo! Stop!"

At the sound of her voice, the chimp halted his attack and jumped into Niki's arms, hugging her and chattering with glee.

"Are you convinced now?" Niki shouted at the troops, explaining how Bobo had been in her father's chambers and she was the only real witness to the assassination. "If you love your country, you will arrest this man for his crime!" she concluded, leveling a finger at Akutu.

"Do not listen!" a voice yelled above the commotion. "Shoot them now!"

The voice was familiar, and the Hardys picked Mantu out of the crowd. He had his gun raised and aimed at Niki!

"Dive!" Joe cried, grabbing the girl and yanking her to the ground along with Bobo.

A single shot rang out, whizzing over their heads.

Then more shots were fired, the whole camp exploding in an uproar as the troops split up in mortal combat—mercenaries against loyalists.

"I'm getting out of here!" Chet yelped, dropping to his hands and knees and scrambling full speed toward the jungle.

Suddenly, war whoops and blazing gunfire broke from the jungle as Bidoli's men stormed into the camp, diverting flying bullets from the escaping youths. Bidoli himself stopped for a moment to make sure the four were unhurt.

"Thanks," Joe panted as he reached the cover of the jungle with Niki and Bobo. "I'm not sure we would've made it."

After giving Niki a quick hug in greeting, Bidoli turned to the boys. "I am the one who should thank you!" he said with a smile. "You will be heroes in my country forever. But now you must go. This is no longer your fight. The jeep is waiting at the crest of the hill. Leave it with Heshee after you retrieve your car."

With that, the Desert Phantom leapt into Akutu's camp with his men and disappeared into the fray. The whole place was now engulfed in a full-scale war!

"Come on!" Frank ordered, taking Niki by the hand and keeping low to avoid stray bullets.

Racing through the jungle, the youths made it to the rim of the hidden valley. Bidoli had parked the jeep under a jungle palm. Niki stared down at the encampment, her arms around Bobo.

"Aren't you coming with us?" Joe asked.

"No, I will stay," she replied softly, still gazing at the raging battle below. "I must be at Bidoli's side when he wins."

The African girl looked at the three boys. "Thank you again." She smiled warmly. "I will remember you always."

"We'll remember you, too," Frank said sincerely. "And I hope everything turns out all right."

"It will," Niki spoke, her voice soft but without a trace of doubt. "It will."

It was hard for the boys to leave her, but at her insistence they finally parted and drove off. Chet had given Bobo a final pat and now looked back sadly.

"How about a pet chimp for your birthday?" Frank consoled his forlorn friend. "Would you like that?"

"You couldn't find one like Bobo," Chet murmured. "Just like it won't be easy to find a friend like Niki again."

The boys headed north over the mountains to the desert, then turned west until they reached the rented Landrover they had left outside Zebwa.

They knew they would never see Niki Jerusa again!

15 Super Van

"Shouldn't you two be doing your homework, or are you such hot-shots now you can forget all about things like school and grades?"

Aunt Gertrude stood at the living-room door with her hands on her hips, sternly appraising her two nephews who were stretched out on the sofa in front of the television.

"In a minute, Aunty," Frank responded, not taking his eyes from the set. "We want to see this report."

Three months had gone by since their trip to Zebwa, and the evening news was broadcasting a special report on the small African nation.

"Here it comes," Joe said, leaning forward.

Joe turned up the volume to make sure they didn't miss a word. The brothers watched as an aerial view of the mountain range appeared on the screen.

"That's where we were!" Joe beamed at his aunt, who had sat down in an armchair. "Those are the mountains we crossed."

"Shhhh!" Frank hushed his younger brother. "I want to hear."

The image was replaced by a shot of Zebwa's capital city, then the camera zoomed in on the presidential palace. A newscaster stood outside, microphone in hand.

"Zebwa has been wracked by strife, famine, and terrorism ever since the bloody rebel overthrow and the assassination of its president over two years ago," the man began. "But today, it is calm again and back on the road to recovery, with President Bidoli in control and the former president's daughter, Niki Jerusa, at his side."

The newscaster described how the loyalist forces, led by the Desert Phantom, had overthrown the Tota rebels and regained power. There was no mention of Akutu or the Hardys.

"They could at least give you *some* credit," Aunt Gertrude grumbled when the report was over. "After all, if it hadn't been for you, that girl would be dead now and that horrible bald general would be president."

"It's enough that *you're* proud of us." Frank winked. "What more glory could we ask for?"

Just then the phone rang and Joe went to pick it up. It was Chet.

"Did you see that thing about Zebwa on the news?" Chet asked excitedly.

"You bet," Joe replied. "I guess Bobo's back home again, safe and sound."

"Be serious!" Chet stammered indignantly. "I'm glad Bobo's okay, but the important thing is that Niki finally has the chance to do something about all those starving people! I think it's great!"

"So do I," Joe said. "Say, why don't we get together after school tomorrow and celebrate? We can go to Arnie's."

Arnie's was a luncheonette near Bayport High where the boys often gathered after classes.

"Sounds excellent!" Chet agreed. "See you then."

"Don't hang up yet," Joe said. "I want to ask your sister to come, too."

"Sure. She's right here."

Iola had been angry when Joe had left the night of the beauty contest, and she'd begun dating Jim Gunther out of spite. But after Joe's return from Africa, they had made up, especially since Joe had helped her win the college scholarship after all by taking Niki away.

"Can you be there?" Joe asked Iola.

"I wouldn't miss it!" Iola exclaimed. "I mean, how many girls have heroes for boyfriends?"

When Joe was off the phone, Frank called his own girlfriend, Callie Shaw, to invite her along, too.

The next day after school, the whole group met at Arnie's to celebrate the liberation of Zebwa.

"To Niki!" Frank hailed, raising his glass.

"To Niki!" the others cheered.

Just then, Fenton Hardy walked in and joined the group. "I picked this up from the post office," he said, handing Frank a letter. "It came registered and it's for you."

"It's from Zebwa!" Frank exclaimed and quickly tore the letter open. Inside was a note from Niki and a check made out to Frank and Joe.

"Twenty thousand dollars!" Frank gasped. "She sent us twenty thousand dollars!"

A hush of silence fell over the group as they all stared at Frank in awe. He read Niki's letter aloud. She was recounting what had happened since the boys had left. Frank read on, "There is much work to be done, but I am very happy. I hope this money will help you get the super van you told me about. I miss you and think of you often. Love, Niki. P.S. Bobo misses you, too!"

Frank looked at his father. "We can't accept the money!" he said.

Mr. Hardy nodded, proud that his sons had resisted the temptation to turn professional. "I know. But I have an idea what you can do with it to put it to good use!"

Several days later, Frank, Joe, and many of their friends were assembled at the Hardys' home.

"Now what's the big surprise you have for us?" Phil Cohen demanded after almost everyone had arrived.

"It's out back," Frank said and led the way through the kitchen door. In the driveway stood a dark blue police van! They'd be needing it sooner than anyone could imagine. They'd be bringing it with them to Florida to help them solve *The Skyfire Puzzle*.

"It's not new and it needs a paint job," Joe explained, "but it's in top running condition."

"Wow!" Chet cried out. "How'd you get it?"

"We donated the twenty thousand dollars to the police charity fund for homeless children, so Chief Collig gave us this surplus van they were going to auction off. Isn't it great?"

"It sure is," Chet cried and kicked a tire.

"The chief promised he'd sell us a used police computer and electronic surveillance equipment at a cut-rate price," Joe added. "Wait until we outfit this baby properly. It'll be the greatest thing you've ever seen."

Suddenly, Chet's face fell. "And what do I get?" he asked. "After all, I went to Zebwa, too!"

"You get to ride with us wherever we go, of

156

course," Joe said, smiling. "By the way, Chet, what happened to your instant aquarium deal you cooked up with Heshee? You get any orders yet?"

"Didn't I tell you?" Chet said gloomily. "Heshee can only come up with a dozen eggs a month, if he's lucky. At that rate, I'll never make any money."

"Too bad," Joe remarked. "I thought it was a great idea."

Just then, the boys' friend, Tony Prito, came out the back door. "Hey, Chet!" he called. "I drove by your house to pick you up and your mother gave me this. It had just come in the mail for you."

He handed Chet an envelope and the chubby boy broke into a wide grin. "It's from Niki!" he said and quickly opened it. Out fell a gold ring and a note from the African girl. It said that the ring was the one that Bobo had worn on his finger. "I thought you would like to have it as a memento," Niki concluded.

Chet's eyes lit up as he put the gold band on his little finger. "I love it!" he exclaimed. "It's worth all the super vans in the world!"

THE THREE INVESTIGATORS

Meet the Three Investigators — Jupiter Jones, Pete Crenshaw
and Bob Andrews. Their motto "We Investigate Anything"
leads them into some bizarre and dangerous situations. Join the
boys in a series of sensational mysteries.

Armada

DUEL MASTER

*Experience the ultimate role-playing quest
with the Duelmaster two-player game system*

The Duelmaster series is an exciting development in
gamebooks which allows you to pit your wits against a
real-life opponent. Now TWO players can join together
in the same adventure. Each takes a different book and
strives to avoid defeat at the hand of a friend.

Challenge of the Magi

Secretly make your choice of character – pyromancer,
necromancer, sorceror, druid, wizard or magician.

Arm yourself with powerful magic spells.

Use skill and cunning to outwit your opponent as you
explore the sixteen realms of the Rainbow Land, where-
in lie rich rewards and lethal traps.

Discover the secret artefacts that will enhance your
powers and prepare you for the final combat.

Have YOU got what it takes to triumph in this brilliant
game of ingenuity and chance?

Also available: *Blood Valley*

Armada

Here are some of the most recent titles in our exciting fiction series:

☐ Danger: Due North *J. J. Fortune* £1.75
☐ The Chalet School Triplets
  Elinor M. Brent-Dyer £1.75
☐ Legion of the Dead *J. H. Brennan* £1.95
☐ The Bluebeard Room *Carolyn Keene* £1.75
☐ The Swamp Monster *Franklin W. Dixon* £1.75
☐ The Mystery of the Smashing Glass
  Marc Brandel £1.75
☐ Horse of Fire *Patricia Leitch* £1.75
☐ Cry of a Seagull *Monica Dickens* £1.75

Armadas are available in bookshops and newsagents, but can also be ordered by post.

HOW TO ORDER
ARMADA BOOKS, Cash Sales Dept., GPO Box 29, Douglas, Isle of Man, British Isles. Please send purchase price plus 15p per book (maximum postal charge £3.00). Customers outside the UK also send purchase price plus 15p per book. Cheque, postal or money order – no currency.

NAME (Block letters) _____

ADDRESS_____

_____

_____